MURDER BY SOUP

Andy Jarvis

The following work is fiction, set in the year 1980. The names and places of business are fictional. All characters portrayed in this publication are fictional as are the institutions and their associated characters. Although some of the locations are actual places on the island of Corfu, others are fictional.
The actions and dialogue of the characters are not meant to be representative of the people on the island of Corfu or the resort of Gouvia or of any particular persons living today or in the past or generally representative of any individuals or cultures in any locality in the world. All reasonable efforts have been made to ensure that the characters do not resemble actual persons, living or dead. Any similarity is entirely coincidental.

My thanks go to

Vanessa, for her unbiased advice and valuable critique.

ISBN

978-1-4467-5275-3

This story is made up.
None of the events described ever happened.

The Hotel Aeres, Gouvia Corfu, 1980

It was the best of holidays; it was the worst of holidays. It was the best because the sun poured out its glorious rays for an entire summer and the worst because on the third day one of the hotel guests slumped dead face first into his soup. Now everyone in the dining room that evening thought this was some joke, that's why nobody screamed, gasped, or fainted. You see, the man was something of a joker, prankster and serial complainer. I was first aware of Mr. Barton on the plane some seats back loudly complaining. From the moment we took off from Manchester Airport, to the second we disembarked in Corfu, his voice drifted up the aisle like an annoying itch you can't reach. He complained of the meal, the seats, the in-flight movie and the stewards and stewardesses. So disturbing he was that I couldn't concentrate on the Windsor Davies interview I was reading in the in-flight magazine I found between the lifejacket inflation instructions and the vomit bag. The way things were going one or the other might have found its use.

Anyway, this complaining/joking lasted into the holiday. He poked fun at the Border Patrol officers, the bus courier and the hotel staff. I had sincerely hoped the passport control officials arrest him. Nobody on the plane wanted him. Border Patrol didn't get it. To them he was just another funny Brit making funny noises and laughing at himself. He was clever in that way, saying things indirectly so that the insults went right over their heads. He complained about his hotel room, he swore at the room maids who spoke not a word of English, the family who owned the hotel and the hotel owner's sons who were kind and courteous to the guests. He complained about the food, he complained about the waiter, he complained about the soup. He complained most of all about the waiter who became the brunt of his jokes, mocking and insults. He then dubbed our poor waiter 'Manual.' No, not Manuel, as in the Fawlty Towers waiter. He wouldn't even give him that courtesy. No, he kept calling out 'Manual!' as in instruction manual; saying he always had to 'consult the Manual,' ask the poor man something or other as in: 'Why is this dinner taking so long?' 'Why don't you have any British beer?' 'Why is this soup cold?' 'Why do I always have to consult the 'Manual?''

So, on this third day eyes rolled as Mr. Dave Barton, stood up after complaining about the time he had to wait for his starter in the dining room, enacted the Basil Fawlty silly walk and slapped our poor waiter Tobias on the back of the head Basil Fawlty style. The soup was promptly brought to the table, Barton took two sips, appeared to choke and gasp, tried to stand, failed to and slumped forward face first into his bowl. Now we all thought this was another of Mr. Barton's tantrums, demonstrating the soup was so cold he could stick his face in it. There was some tittering through the dining room, but mostly groans of disapproval. By this time we were all fed up of the antics. I admit the soup was something of a paradox, it being listed on the menu with correct names such as minestrone, mushroom etc., but none of the names matched the appearance or consistency of the soups. The said mushroom looked for all the world like tomato, the farmhouse vegetable like pea and ham etc. This was anathema to our Mr. Barton. It was more than all he needed to kick up such a fuss over what was obviously and simply a misunderstood menu mismatch. I pretended to ignore, but was immediately aware something was very wrong when I took my first spoonful of the soup expecting it to be less than warm and scalded my tongue. I got up and walked over to Barton's table. His face was still in the soup. I stuck my finger in the bowl. It was red hot like mine.

'I believe someone should call an ambulance,' I said.

Then there was a scream. Then there were gasps. Then there was a faint.

Some of the guests gathered around Barton's table, others drifted out of the room. The hotel owner, Mrs. Samaras, came out from the kitchen with an angry scowl across her face and was about to lift Barton's head out.

I shook my head. 'You'd best not touch him.'

2.

Dave Barton was dead. Nobody announced it officially, but a guy who can sit with his face in a red hot bowl of soup is at least unconscious and at worst has no neural activity sending pain signals powerful enough to wake him. That and the fact that the ambulance crew threw him unceremoniously onto a stretcher with his face covered. Not everyone in the dining room saw his face, some having left when they realised it was no joke. I couldn't tell if it was the minestrone of the day or gently broiled face skin. I guessed it was some of each. Those chopped vegetables that clung onto his cheeks when he was lifted out weren't exactly acne. The ambulance crew took him away without the urgency of their arrival or sirens.

Apart from the death of a guest, the following day started like any other. It was uncomfortably hot in my first floor room, the mosquitoes had been on rations thanks to window netting and liberal applications of Deet the night before and I had that usual hangover that only time or an English bacon butty can cure. I opened the curtains and netting and let in the morning breeze and sun casting shadows on a blue hotel room patch-worked with light blue paint daubs disguising previously swatted mosquitoes that still showed through the paint. It was still a pleasant room, a comfortable bed, but too hot to use the bedcovers, hence the Deet. The room reminded me of a Cezanne painting, not so much artful, but distorted planes. I had a bedside table where only two legs touched the floor at any given time, depending on where you shifted the water pitcher and basin. Those were for decoration. Even in 1980 everywhere had sinks and running water. Apart from that it was basic like a nineteenth century bedroom. A functional dark varnished wardrobe with ornate brass handles, matching chest of drawers and a few wall pegs to hang a wet pair of trunks and towel and a single wicker chair if you can't be bothered to hang up on wall pegs. It was rustic, no TV and pleasant. Just me and the island. I had an agent back home who suggested the island. The ideal retreat for a writer, he'd said. Stay the whole summer, he'd said. I'd be anonymous, recharge my batteries, I would be inspired, he'd said. Then I'd come back to make him a shed load of money.

He hadn't said.

I picked the accommodation, the Aeres Hotel in Gouvia. I could afford more and the agent was willing to contribute, but this is what I wanted, a retreat away from the pretentious wealthy who only talked about their wealth. That was something the agent didn't get. Once someone starts harking on about their yacht, their big home, their investments, you can't get them out of your head. On the map, Gouvia seemed right, a small village near the sea, a handful of bars and a hotel with a seawater pool. Ideal for people like me who don't float.

I paid a quick small room visit, washed my face and looked in the mirror, deciding I'd bypass the shave for a time when I felt more awake. A fifty-five year old unfit writer stared back. Things could be worse, I thought. I was on an idyllic island where I was anonymous and nobody cared if I was old or clean-shaven, whereas I could be back home sat under a shelter licking ice cream on the Blackpool promenade in the rain. Then I'd feel like a fifty-five year old unfit writer.

Downstairs in the dining room things were a little cooler. A big overhead fan creaked and whished the air and insects towards open full length windows where red and yellow floral curtains fluttered in and out with the breeze. A few guests were down for breakfast. Some smiled their good mornings, others seemed understandably glum from the previous night's event. I sat at a table by myself and ordered tea. The unfortunate waiter Tobias, the victim of Dave Barton's abuse served me. I asked if he was okay that morning. He laid out fresh, warm croissants, butter, jam and a thick slice of Madeira cake. He poured tea from a nice white teapot, patterned with terracotta Greek warriors that looked like they were two nil down against the Cyclops.

'With respect, sir, I do not wish to talk about it.'

'No, I don't suppose you do. Sorry I brought it up.'

Tobias smiled and left for the kitchen and more breakfasts. There was a young couple at the next table. The girl leaned over. 'Have you heard any news about Mr. Barton?'

'He's dead,' I said. 'I don't suppose I have to tell you that. Don't tell me you miss him already?'

'No, I must admit things will be more peaceful without him, but such a terrible way to go.'

'What way? Nobody said how he died.'

'I mean slumped forward with his face in a bowl of soup,' said the girl. 'So undignified.'

'I don't think Barton did dignity. I think if he had a choice that might have been one of the ways he'd have liked to go. Maybe it should be written on his epitaph.'

'That's not very funny,' said the girl's young man friend.

'It wasn't meant to be. Barton was the comedian, not me. I only say it as I see it.'

'Rude,' said the girl.

'Look, I'm truly sorry he's dead, but I can't lament. Unfortunately, people like Barton bring out the worst in me.'

They went quiet after that and finished breakfast. I finished mine and took off for the day, wandering the beach and skimming stones on the sea. I lay in the sun on a sandy bit of a mostly stony beach, watching a man casting a net from shore in a part of the water where a stream flowed into it from the woods behind. I'd heard somewhere that mackerel liked the shore where streams ran. They wallowed in the silt they deposited apparently. I knew people like that, mostly in the publishing world.

I came back for the evening meal. The Aeres' owner, Mrs. Samaras – who insisted everyone call her Elena – was a widower with two sons. There was Christos, 22 years old, strikingly good looking with oddly blue eyes (I previously thought all Mediterranean folk were brown-eyed) and built more like a navvy than a waiter. I asked him how he looked like a navvy from lifting dishes and he asked me what one was. When I explained the historical side in constructing great buildings and digging out canals back home in the industrial revolution he seemed quite proud, flexed a bicep and told me he was a navvy – of sorts. 'I'm building a house,' he said, which surprised me. 'Not really building. Doing up, as you English say, on my days off.' And then there was Philo, 15, equally as handsome and elusive outside of working hours when things ran like clockwork in the dining room. 'He's still at school,' explained Elena. 'We let him study as much as he wants. He wishes to be a scientist.'

Elena alerted each of us as we entered the dining room that the police had dropped by, checking the guests passports stored in the reception room safe. The police had asked to be informed if anyone requested checking out early. They'd hung onto the passports in the meantime.

I took off for a couple of days then. I couldn't stand the thought of all those wagging tongues, amateur sleuths and conspiracy theories. I'd had a belly full of that back home. Everyone wants to tell a crime writer his business. I just wanted to empty my head for once. I grabbed breakfast in a remote corner of the dining room and disappeared until after the evening meal, wandering the coast road, catching buses to remote villages in the hills, drinking reasonable beer in quiet taverns and open air beach bars and thinking about nothing but pine trees, white beaches and blue sky. I was no more inclined to write as a sloth wanted to run a marathon.

One morning there were two additions and one missing

from breakfast. Tobias was nowhere to be seen, but two policemen certainly were to be seen. You couldn't miss them, near the dining room entrance and right by the kitchen door, a uniformed officer and another in casual wear. I gathered the casually dressed one was also a cop, a senior one on a case, or what we call 'plainclothes.' Both were drinking coffee and eating cake and croissants, the casual one in khaki short sleeves, black slacks and black Doc Martin's (or the Greek equivalent) He was a portly, balding guy with some remaining suspiciously black hair and grey eyebrows, late-forties, I guessed and puffed on a fat cigar through a suspiciously matching black moustache. Think Greek version of William Conrad, aka Frank Cannon, only he forgot to touch up the eyebrows. The smoke caught the ceiling fan and my nostrils. He beckoned me to sit, so I sat. Elena was unusually silent as she served me tea and croissants. I poured tea but didn't eat. The cigar cop introduced himself as Elias Castellanos, a chief detective and divisional head of Corfu police. I guessed his rank was the equivalent of an Inspector. His partner was a younger fair-haired guy, with a square jaw and dumb face, whose name I soon forgot because it was too hard to get my tongue around it. The name started with an 'E' and I think ended in 'O and S' and probably had every vowel of the alphabet in between. I called him Deet, as he looked like he was only there to keep the flies off Castellanos.

Castellanos' first question floated out of the moustache on a foul plume of cigar smoke. 'And your name is?'

'Fox,' I said. 'Angelo Fox.' I felt uncomfortable in his presence and was tempted to add "pleased to meet you," even though I wasn't.

'Very good, Mr. Fox. And I see you are here on Corfu on holiday from England?'

'Me and a few thousand other Brits. It's what we do when it pisses down with rain back home.'

'Yes, very good,' said Castellanos. 'The weather is not so good in England, I know. I have cousins who live and work there. Restaurant business, you know.'

'I bet they're always writing and telling you how much they love the weather.'

'Very good again. It's true what they say about the English. They make up for the sadness of poor climate with bright humour. You English think everything is humorous, even death.'

'It wasn't meant as humour and it wasn't bright.'

Castellanos eyed me for a moment and glanced at my untouched food. He puffed and blew another billow, respectfully away to his left and disrespectfully in the direction of the other diners. He didn't like the English and I could tell. This was about Barton. But I didn't want to know about Barton. I'd had enough of Barton on the plane, in the hotel, everywhere. I swear I'd even heard his obnoxious voice drift over from one tavern to the other in that peaceful place, soiling the air like industrial soot once soiled English buildings. Castellanos was humouring me, that was obvious and the word 'death' was dropped into the conversation intentionally. He was looking for a response, a kneejerk reaction. He was playing a mind game that reminded me of my own fiction and I didn't like that. I came away wanting to forget about that.

'Tell me Mr. Fox,' said Castellanos. 'What is your business back in England?'

'I'm a writer.'

'A writer?' Castellanos grey eyebrows raised. 'You are a journalist?' He shot a glance at Deet. Publicity wasn't his thing, apparently.

'Novelist,' I said. 'I write fiction.'

'Fiction?' He sounded relieved. 'What sort of fiction?'

'Crime fiction. I write murder mysteries.'

Castellanos looked at Deet again, then at me. 'I see. Then

this case must be of some interest to you?'

'This case? What case? I don't know what you mean.'

'I can disclose to you sir, that we believe that the deceased of your party, Mr. Barton, was murdered.'

'He's the last person I'd want at any party of mine. And why would that be of interest to me?'

'Perhaps this is a story for you?'

I didn't know if this was a question or an accusation. 'I don't want a story. I just want some peace, quiet and beer. I'm like anyone else here. I want to get away from the day job.'

'Can you think of anyone who might have had motivation to cause harm to Mr. Barton?'

'How about everyone in the hotel? Barton was a pain in the backside and no one liked him.'

'I see,' said Castellanos. 'That will be all for now.'

'How did he die?' I asked.

Castellanos looked at his partner again, who got a notebook out from his shirt pocket and scribbled a few words. Or maybe he drew a cartoon for all I knew. He didn't look bright enough for joined up writing. Castellanos blew another disrespectful plume of cigar, towards the kitchen this time just as Elena came through. The smoke followed her slipstream as she breezed across the dining room floor with two trays of breakfasts.

'We will not disclose this for the moment, sir.'

'Charming.' I drained my cup, got up and left the food behind. Cigar smoke ruins my appetite almost as much as idiot cops. I headed up to my room, changed into trunks, grabbed a towel and wandered across the Aeres' gravel forecourt, through a fretwork arch of red hibiscus in full bloom to the pool. Castellanos questioning had inexplicably tired me and I felt like a snooze near some salt water without a beach.

The pool was quiet and I was alone, just how I wanted it. I slipped in feet first and lay on my back floating, buoyed by the density of its salt content, fed by pipeline from the nearby bay. I tried not to imagine what else might be in the water, so I stopped thinking about it and about anything and just floated, kept up by barely moving arms and legs. I watched the odd plane overhead coming into Corfu International a few miles away. I swam a little, lay on a lounger and slept a while until my trunks dried then had a beer in Niko's Tavern a short walk away.

Across the road from Niko's a stage was being set up in a large open area between the pine trees. I asked Niko. Political rally, he told me. Great. As long as they were shouting in Greek and didn't go on past midnight I didn't care. I had another beer, left a tip on the table and wandered back to the hotel for a shower.

Upstairs in my room a pleasant breeze filtered through the mosquito netting carrying scents of hibiscus, passiflora and pine tree tinged with a whiff of cigar.

3.

I didn't mind that Castellanos had been snooping in my room. That's what coppers do and Greek coppers had no reason to be any different. What I did mind was that he didn't seem to want to hide the fact. Things had been shifted about, the wobbly set of drawers had been left open and my clothes in the wardrobe seemed to be out of order. And he left his scent, like a cat pisses on bushes he wanted me to know. He was making a statement for sure. I dismissed it and had my shower, changed into clean tropical design Bermudas, white shirt, sandals, straw trilby with a fishing fly pinned on its blue band and wandered into Gouvia village for a couple more beers before returning for the evening meal.

The fare that evening was omelette, a side salad of giant sliced plum tomatoes and cucumber, beef stew and chips and something brown and wobbly for dessert that the couple at the next table told me was crème caramel.

I noticed Tobias was still absent and only Elena's sons were serving the guests. I mentioned it to Elena as she served the brown wobblies.

'Tobias not here anymore.' She sounded sad.

'Oh. Did he get another job somewhere?'

'No, no job. He gone.'

'Where to?'

She disappeared into the kitchen for more deserts. When she'd served these she came back to my table. 'I don't wish to talk about Tobias. I too upset to say now.'

I ate up, went out for a few more beers at the local taverns and turned it over in my mind about Tobias disappearing. My writing brain was kicking in against my will. It didn't take much to come up with some story ideas and Castellanos could be fitted into all of them. Shady coppers always worked in fiction. Greek ones could make it interestingly different. I had a Metaxa and tonic nightcap served by Christos back at the Aeres bar. I was tempted to ask about Tobias' absence, but I didn't think Christos was any more willing to talk about it than his mum Elena. And she didn't want to talk about it. I had an uneasy night's sleep.

In the morning I wandered into Gouvia after breakfast and bought a two day old English newspaper from a corner katástima, then hit the pool for a swim, a catch-up nap and catch-up on home news. Poolside was empty so I swam a bit, towelled and fell into a short nap on a lounger with a copy of The Daily Star shielding my face. Apart from trashy romance novels, half of which were written in German, that's all the reading material they had in the store. Apparently the Greeks think us Brits like trashy gossip, Barbara Cartland and sensationalism.

When I awoke I pulled the newspaper from my face, sat up, drank tepid water from a plastic bottle, pulled on my sunglasses and lay back down. Across the pool two elderly ladies had appeared lounging and reading paperbacks. After a while one of them placed her book on the poolside tiles, stretched and appeared to doze. The other lady kept reading, but also kept looking over the top of her book at me. Maybe she wasn't looking at me. It's not easy to tell when someone's wearing sunglasses where they're looking, but she would read – or pretend to – then peek over the top of the book or under it. I couldn't see it for definite, but I was now fairly sure she was looking at me. There wasn't anything else in my direction, an empty pool bar and a cleaner's closet behind me and a few pines, climbing flowers on arch frames and rock walls. I took my sunglasses off, picked my hat up by the lounger and pulled it over my face, pretending to be asleep, but watching back through the straw weave. That's when I knew she was watching me. I couldn't complain, I was after all, watching her. She placed the book in her lap and nudged her friend from her slumber. The friend awoke with a puzzled look. Book lady nodded in my direction and said something that was lost in the breeze hissing through the pines behind me. Her friend looked over then back at book lady. Book lady fingered something in the paperback and pointed in my direction. The friend squinted over the top of her sunglasses at me. They watched me for a few seconds longer, then got up and wandered over.

They both tip-toed by the pool like they didn't want to wake me, but I'd guessed that's exactly what they wanted to do. I pretended to be asleep. It was getting hot inside the straw facemask. The book lady stood over me and cleared her throat. 'Good morning,' she said. 'I'm so sorry to bother you.'

I lifted my hat. Book lady was blocking the sun in a big straw Raffia hat turned up at the front with a red ribbon hanging off the back and wearing huge round sunglasses. She wore a modest red bikini top, and loose shorts with a yellow and red floral design that could hide her by the dining room curtains. She removed the hat like I was someone who needed the respect of a vicar. I could see she might have been blond once upon a time, now turning a shade of mauve. Her friend wore a floral bikini in blue with yellow flowers, the same hat with a blue ribbon and hair that was auburn at least where it showed from the hat rim. I recognised them from the dining room, although I'd never spoken to them before.

'Don't apologise,' I said. 'If I lay here much longer I'll turn into a saddlebag. What can I do for you?'

The book lady removed her sunglasses. She had a pleasant face and green eyes that might have matched Gouvia bay. 'We were just wondering...is it you?'

'Me who?'

'Well…the author.' She held up the paperback. A Most Precise Murder. One I'd written a few years back. Then she turned it over to show yours truly on the back cover. I'd argued this with my agent at the time. I wanted anonymity. He argued that if I was ever to gain real fame, fans wanted to know what their favourite authors look like. I argued they'd know who to kill if they didn't like my writing.

'You're Jimmy Finn,' said the book lady's friend.

The book lady rolled her eyes. 'He's not Jimmy Finn, silly. Jimmy Finn is the detective he writes about. He's Angelo Fox…aren't you?'

'And who are you?'

'Oh, I'm sorry,' said the book lady. 'I'm Madge and this is my friend Mabel. We're here on holiday.'

'I never would have guessed.'

Madge clapped her hands. 'Oh silly me, of course you know that. It is you though, isn't it? I've read most of your books, I mean we both read your books and this is the first one that has your photo on it. I brought it with me on holiday and I've just started reading it today. I was reading the back cover and saw your face for the first time and realised that you're that nice looking man who sits all by himself at meal times and then I, I mean we, realised it must be you.'

It seemed pointless denying it and they seemed harmless enough. 'Yeah, you got me. Well done, ladies, Jimmy Finn himself couldn't have tracked me down quicker.'

'Ooh, fabulous!' said Madge. 'Right here in our own hotel! Isn't that fabulous, Mabel? Angelo Fox in our hotel! Oh, this is going to be such a fabulous holiday!'

'Oh, just fabulous!' repeated Mabel. 'I'll be awake all night now just thinking about it!'

'Mabel gets insomnia you know,' said Madge.

'Alright Madge, that's quite enough of that. I'm sure Jimmy…I mean Mr. Fox doesn't need to know. It's just so exciting though!'

'And how long are you two lovely ladies staying here?' I asked.

'Oh, did you hear that, Mabel?' said Madge. 'He called us lovely ladies. What a charming man.'

'A charming man,' repeated Mabel. 'Just like Jimmy Finn. He's such a charming man and so clever.'

'A few weeks,' said Madge. 'Maybe longer if the weather stays fine. We're on an open flight and Mrs. Samaras, I mean Elena, has said she'll keep a booking open for us. You see, we've nothing to hurry back home for. We're both...' Madge held her hand up to her mouth and coughed: 'Retired. And I'm a widower and Mabel is divorced. Such a horrible man he was, wasn't he, Mabel?'

'A horrible man,' repeated Mabel. 'Not like Jimmy Finn at all. Not like you Mr. Fox. Such a charming man.'

My heart sank. I had a few weeks to go. I could move hotel. That wouldn't do my image any good if the two ladies thought I was avoiding them. Word might get out that Jimmy Finn was a snob. 'Look, you two are very nice ladies and I'm sure you could do me a small favour, could you?'

'Of course we could,' said Madge.

'Of course we could,' repeated Mabel.

'Don't let on who I am,' I said. 'I mean don't go telling the other hotel guests who I really am. I'm here to forget who I am myself, you understand. Sometimes I just want to get away from the whole Jimmy Finn aura and chill out. I came here to relax, swill beer, swim, hike, sunbathe, sleep and swill beer and not write. I don't want to even think about Jimmy Finn. Enjoy your holiday, enjoy the book, I hope Jimmy gives you a few good thrills and spills, but please do me this one favour, okay?'

'Oh, of course we will,' said Madge. She bent forward and tapped the side of her nose twice. 'Mum's the word. We won't say a thing, will we Mabel?'

'Oh, not a thing,' said Mabel. 'Anything for you, Mr. Fox. Anything at all we can do, we will do it. Anything.'

'And when Mabel says anything, Mr. Fox, she does mean anything.' Madge nudged her friend.

'Call me Angelo,' I said. 'Just don't shout it out in the dining room.'

'Oh, you hear that, Mabel? We can call him Angelo. Isn't that fabulous?'

'Fabulous!' repeated Mabel, clapping her hands.

'And won't Mrs. Fox mind us being on first name terms?' Madge asked.

'I'm not married. There is no Mrs. Fox.'

'Oh, really,' said Madge. 'I can't believe that. Can you believe that, Mabel?

'I can't believe that,' said Mabel. 'Such a shame. A nice polite, charming man like yourself and no Mrs. Fox? Are you like Madge and I, then? Was there once a Mrs. Fox?'

'That's enough now, Mabel,' said Madge. 'We mustn't pry into Angelo's life. We should leave you in peace now, shouldn't we, Mabel?'

'Oh, of course,' said Mabel. 'Silly me and my big gob. We should go, there's that musician on at Upsilon's bar later. We're going to the shops first and then getting ready for the performance this afternoon. Such a shame though, all alone on holiday. But if you ever want us to show you around the island, well Madge and I have been coming here for years.'

'Thanks. I appreciate the offer, but I'll be fine ladies.' I said.

Such a shame, though,' said Madge.

'And such a shame about poor Tobias,' said Mabel.

'What...what?' I sat up and threw my legs over the lounger. 'What about Tobias?'

'Why, haven't you heard?' said Madge. 'The police took him away. We think it must be something to do with that awful Mr. Barton.'

I'd missed this news. It's what you get when you disappear trying to avoid other guests. This was one missed snippet that someone like Jimmy Finn would laugh at me about. 'How do you know about this? I asked about Tobias and Mrs. Samaras wouldn't tell me anything.'

'Well,' said Madge. 'Mabel overheard Elena crying in the kitchen late one evening as we were passing to our room. Normally we wouldn't eavesdrop, would we Mabel?'

'Oh no, we don't eavesdrop,' said Mabel. 'But when we heard Tobias' name mentioned, we became intrigued. She was talking to her sons about Tobias being arrested.'

'How do you know what she was saying?' I asked. 'She always orders the boys around in Greek.'

'Mabel speaks Greek,' said Madge.

'I went to night classes just for it,' said Mabel. 'It's so nice to be able to talk to the locals in their own language and we come here so often it only seemed right. Such wonderful people, the Greeks and so much history.'

'Yeah, yeah,' I said. 'But what about Tobias?'

'Well that's all we know,' said Madge. 'He was taken into custody. He must be a suspect in Mr. Barton's death. They do think it's murder, you know. That's what that awful policeman said. Horrible man with his foul-smelling cigars and impertinent questions. It's like he thought we were involved.'

'Horrible man,' repeated Mabel.

'And I can't believe for one minute that Tobias could be capable of murder,' said Madge, 'if that's what the police think. Such a sweet man, Tobias. And that awful Mr. Barton treated him so disrespectfully.'

'Maybe that's your motive,' I said.

'You'd think so, wouldn't you,' said Mabel. 'But if that's why the police have arrested him, we think they've jumped on the first innocent suspect for their own convenience.'

'Making life easy for themselves,' said Madge. 'And how

could poor Tobias have possibly murdered him? There was no knife or gun or anything. I think Mr. Barton had a heart attack, that's all. I just hope someone finds out the truth soon and lets him go. I mean, what would Jimmy Finn do in such a situation?'

'Ooh, now that's a thought,' said Mabel. 'What *would* Jimmy Finn do? An innocent man banged up in prison...'

'Now wait a minute, ladies,' I said. 'We don't know exactly what Tobias has been arrested for. You're jumping to conclusions here. Maybe he hasn't paid his taxes for all we know.'

'Oh, silly,' said Madge. 'Nobody in Greece pays taxes.'

'That's a myth,' I said.

'I know, but that's what people say. But what would Jimmy Finn do?'

'Look, Jimmy Finn is fiction. He lives in my head and right now he's on furlough down at the tavern drinking beer.'

'But aren't you curious?' said Madge. 'Couldn't you find out what he's been arrested for?'

'Oh yes, please!' said Mabel. 'Oh, could you, Mr. Fox? Please...we're so concerned about Tobias, such a lovely man. And I'm sure Elena is just as worried about him. Please Mr. Fox.'

'Angelo,' I said. 'Call me Angelo. If I'm going to visit the guy in custody I'll square it with Elena first. I'm sure she'll be overjoyed about you overhearing her discussing her misery with her sons.'

'Oh thank you, Angelo!' said Madge. 'Such a gentleman, just like Jimmy Finn!'

'Just like Jimmy Finn!' repeated Mabel.

The rest of the morning was spent with me being photographed with Mabel by the pool, then by the floral arch, then by the pool again with the floral arch and the Aeres hotel in the background, then with Madge by me by the pool, then with Madge by the pool again with the floral arch and hotel background again, then all three of us photographed by a hotel guest by the pool, in front of the floral arch, in front of the hotel, under the pines on one leg waving Raffia hats and smiling insanely.

In the afternoon I wandered into town and drank a lot of beer.

4.

The next morning I caught the 10:30 bus into Corfu Town, a picturesque journey taking in colourful farmsteads and dusty olive and lemon groves. I had a carrier bag holding a Tupperware box of Elena's home baked baklava on my knee with the instruction to keep it flat. That was tricky on a bus that bumped along the irregular tarmac, but the journey wasn't too unpleasant. Heady scents of wildflower and dry grasses fought with the diesel fume that drifted in the open windows. I seemed to be the only English person on board, sat alongside Greeks on their way to markets or other businesses. I felt a little out of place, having dressed up as formally as I could for a prison visit in a hot country, wearing light tan shorts, pale blue short sleeves and comfortable Eastland casuals, the ones that have the squiggly laces for some reason.

From the bus depot I took a walk out to the old Palaio Frourio Kerkyras fortress, an old prison, now a museum. I was pleased they didn't use it as a prison anymore. The place was an interesting black hole which I didn't particularly intend visiting, but I needed time to clear my head of alcohol and think about what I was going to say to Tobias. I next had a wander along the harbour front. Corfu looked a smart town on the face of it. The municipal buildings painted in light shades of terracotta, powder blue and lemon stood out proudly in the midday sun and suggested great wealth and investment for some lucky Greeks. It didn't suggest that Madge's remark about no Greeks paying taxes was right. I had thought that was as much a Greek myth as Perseus decapitating Medusa, but the size and number of luxury yachts in dock made me wonder if some knew the system loopholes.

I'd quietly taken Elena to one side that morning after breakfast and squared the visit to Tobias. She was keen on me going, and not too annoyed after I'd explained how I found out about his arrest from Madge and Mabel. She urged me not to let the news spread any further. It was bad for the Aeres hotel image she explained. I couldn't think of anything worse. A guest dropping dead was bad. A staff member getting arrested worse. Elena wanted to see Tobias herself, but the running of the hotel came first. The last time she left the boys in charge a band of some revellers from a new holiday club called 18–30 decided to detour a pub crawl through the hotel bar, bringing a barrage of complaints from the guests. Such nice kids at home, I bet.

I turned inland from the harbour, following a map, taking a few backstreets and alleyways where flaking paint on wood and walls and missing render showed the stonework where the renderer either ran out of render, cement, paint, money or all of them. It must have really pissed some of them, seeing all those yachts just a stone's throw away. The walk took me around nearly a full circle, not far from the bus station where I'd started, to a razor wired rotunda wall surrounding an imposing building on a hill, the Prison of Corfu.

By contrast the old Courthouse at the front where Tobias was being held was a pleasant looking affair. Light terracotta facade with exposed redbrick arches said more of a tavern where a smiling waiter would greet you with an aperitif, a clean table and a smile that said he wanted a good tip. I got a surly duty officer with a look that said he didn't like his siesta disturbing or the English.

He spent half an hour filling in forms in Greek and English that I had to sign. The English ones were translated so badly they might as well have been Greek. He frisked me, emptied my pockets, wallet, hotel key, loose change and took my shoelaces. These went into a plastic tray which I also signed for. He opened the carrier bag and lifted out the Tupperware, pulled the lid off the baklava and had a good sniff and poke round, licking his fingers after.

'Very nice. You buy?'

'Mrs. Samaras homemade. From the Aeres hotel. She bakes the best baklava in Corfu, I am told. I'm sure Tobias will save you a slice if you ask him nicely. For me, you can have the whole boxful. I don't like anything that makes me lick fingers.'

He looked at me strangely, like he couldn't figure out if I'd made a joke or sarcastic comment about his picking around Elena's gift.

'I just don't like it,' I said. 'Too sticky and sweet.'

He had one last look, snapped the lid back on, handed it back to me like an Army sergeant hands a rifle back to a private stood to attention. He put the carrier bag in the tray of my belongings. 'No bags inside the cell.'

He led me off through a barred steel door down a brightly lit hall past a row of suspiciously silent cells. Nobody yelled, jeered, whistled or banged tin cups. Maybe I watch too many prison movies. Maybe it was because there were no bars and they couldn't see me. Tobias' cell was number 4, near the far end.

'Twenty minutes,' the duty officer said.

'Can I go in?'

'Yes. Your risk. He is murderer you understand?'

'So you say. I'll chance it.'

He unlocked the door and I went in, the door behind shut with a clank and screech of key turning. I wondered what exactly I'd signed before entering. The cell wasn't that bad. A little cramped, basic with a pull down wall bed, chair, flushing toilet, sink and not too much graffiti scratched into the concrete. If it was a room in the Aeres I'd probably complain about the size.

Tobias swung his legs over the side of the bed, stood up and embraced me. 'Mister Fox! I am so pleased to see you. There has been a terrible mistake.'

'I hope so, Tobias.' I stood back and looked him up and down. 'You look terrible. They feeding you alright? Here, a little present from Mrs. Samaras.' I handed him the Tupperware.

He pulled the lid back. 'Ah, Elena, she knows how much I love her baklava. Yes, Mr. Fox, they are feeding me, but how can I eat?' He looked down at the baklava with a sorrowful face. 'I could not even eat Elena's baklava, I am so worried. I worry about the family, the Aeres, everything. I worry that the family think I am criminal.'

'They don't,' I said. 'They don't think you're a criminal and they are just as worried about you. Elena sends her love with the baklava and would be here if she could. You know she would, Tobias, she's as fond of you as one of her boys. She's hoping to slip by sometime between mealtimes and the hotel work. You know how much there is to do, even more so without your help at the Aeres.'

'Yes, of course. You tell Elena I will see her soon. This is a mistake, I am certain.'

'What they got you in for? I heard something, but I don't go on rumours, especially those I find hard to believe.'

Tobias placed the baklava on the chair and sat back on the bed burying his face in his hands. His shoulders quivered and I guessed he was sobbing and doing a good job of doing it silently. Then he looked up at me. 'They say I murdered Mr. Barton. But no, I am no murderer. Mr. Barton was horrible to me, but I could not do such a thing, even to him.'

'So how do they say you did it?'

'This I cannot understand,' said Tobias. 'They don't tell me. So they want me to confess first, like they are not sure how I'm supposed to murder. They try to trick me, they say to me 'tell us how you did it and we consider freeing you.' But how can I confess how I murder when I don't murder? I worry about going up the hill, as they say. The big prison on the hill.

You will have seen it, I am sure. This is a nice holding cell they tell me, but the prison is hell. They tell me stories to frighten me into confession. They tell me life will be bad for me in there, bad people who don't care if I'm guilty or not. They say the other prisoners will beat anyone who says they are innocent. But they will see. Maybe Mr. Barton died of heart attack or they will find the real murderer soon, I am certain. Tell this to Elena.'

We had our twenty minutes that seemed like ten, embraced again and the duty cop took me back to the reception area where an ugly sight greeted me. Detective Castellanos portly frame sat with one leg on the floor and half an ass on the edge of the desk soiling the air with cigar. Deet sat on a chair next to him scribbling again in his notebook.

'Good day, Mr. Fox,' said Castellanos.

'It was,' I replied. 'I was just leaving.'

'So what brings you to see the suspect Teresi?'

'Tobias, you mean? I never knew his surname until the duty officer told me. We're all on first name terms at the Aeres. Friends, you see? Elena Samaras, Tobias, the boys Christos and Philo. We all get on like a house on fire. Elena sent me. She's worried about her favourite employee. He's like another son to her and can't believe what's going on. Me neither, as a matter of fact. She's coming to see him soon, when she's less busy. What about you? You going to tell Tobias what he's done, or just make him sweat some more?'

'I have come to interview him, yes,' said Castellanos. 'He will tell us exactly how he did it in time. We already know, but it will go easier for him in trial if he confesses by his own choice. His treatment at the hands of this obnoxious English hotel guest will be considered. The jury will sympathise. So many good citizens of Corfu have experience of you English and your bad manners and bad humour. And as for you, Mr. Fox, I know all about you, the famous writer. This is not your real name, is it? Why did you change your name to Angelo Fox?'

'William Shakespeare was already taken.'

'Don't try to humour me, Mr. Fox. You changed your name. Why?'

'It was my agent's idea to have a pseudonym, an author's name. Derek Plumpton doesn't look too bright on the cover of a paperback. I liked the name Angelo Fox so much I changed it by Deet poll.'

Deet glanced up at me like he'd read my secret poke. 'You mean deed poll,' he said. 'The word is deed, I believe.'

'Yeah, that's what I said.'

'Deet is a mosquito repellent.'

'Yeah, that's right, a British product. Funny you should know that, you'll probably find a can of it in every room back at the hotel.'

Castellanos stubbed his cigar in a brass ashtray and crossed his arms. 'You don't have to play games, Mr. Fox. I can assure you that we have nothing to hide. All the guests' passports were checked and their rooms examined. We have every right in a murder case and Mrs. Samaras was very cooperative. There was only one room where we found what we suspected. That room was Tobias Teresi's.'

'So what did you find?'

'Hidden away under a loose floorboard we found a small phial. Obviously the guilty one didn't want us to find it. The phial contained a small amount of poison. It was identified as strychnine. Not much, but certainly more than enough to kill Mr. Barton outright and possibly more, if the guilty wanted to. The same poison was identified in Mr. Barton's soup he consumed that night. Nowhere else, just in Mr. Barton's serving. Nothing was found anywhere else in the hotel, not even in the kitchen. Only in Teresi's room and in Mr. Barton's soup. The poison must have been placed deliberately in one person's soup. That is murder, not accident. And Tobias Teresi will tell us all about it…in time.'

'Tell me something, Mr. Castellanos,' I said. 'Did you pull up the floorboards in my room?'

'There was no need, Mr. Fox. We had already found the poison and the poisoner.'

'Yeah, it's almost like you figured that out before you started looking.'

Castellanos stood up sharply and snapped his fingers. Deet stood up like an obedient dog, shoving his notebook into his shirt pocket. Castellanos pointed at me directly. 'We are done here, Mr. Fox. I am tired of your 'crime writer's' overactive mind. Make up any story you want for you and your 'agent' and your readers, but it will still only be just that. A story. In the meantime I have a man with a guilty conscience to interview. Goodbye.'

I'd got my writing hat on again. I came to Corfu to get away from that, but Castellanos had firmly placed it there against my will and sent ideas racing through my head. I had a couple of beers in a waterfront tavern to wash away the cigar fume that had worked its way to the back of my tongue, then caught the 3:30 afternoon bus to Gouvia with an empty carrier bag and empty heart. Tobias was going down, of that I was convinced. And I hadn't even asked if he had a lawyer. What kind of crime writer doesn't even ask about lawyers? But I came to Corfu to get away from that.

Castellanos worried me, but I worried him more it seemed. I knew I shouldn't have made the remarks I did, but Castellanos had the kind of attitude that could bring out the sarcasm in Mother Theresa. Maybe it was coincidence him being at the Courthouse at the same time, maybe not. But there was no doubt I interested him, he researching my writer's background. Somehow I don't think he'd give a damn if I was

31

a love poet. One way or another Castellanos would get the confession he wanted and I had to bite my lip. Castellanos believed I was after an idea for a novel. As long as he thought that I'd be alright.

But things still bothered me. Tobias had every motive to wish harm on Dave Barton. But how and where does a humble waiter rushed off his feet all day get hold of strychnine? It was too late now. Castellanos had his man and even if he'd got the wrong one, any other culprit would be a halfwit to try something like it again now that a sucker was going to do time on his behalf. And I had to admit it. Tobias was a nice guy, but still…I think he could have done it. Every man has his breaking point.

Now came the hard part: letting Elena know her favourite employee was destined for the Big House on Barbwire Hill.

5.

Elena didn't hold back on the waterworks. There was no point trying to sugar coat what seemed the obvious destiny for Tobias. The two sons yelled in disbelief. I could tell they were cursing the police. The name Castellanos was repeated through words that sounded like swearwords even in Greek. We were in the kitchen, still an hour or more before the evening meal. The eldest, Christos, blurted out "bent copper" in English as he brushed by me and out the door into the dining room. He returned a minute later with a Metaxa for Elena. The younger son, Philo, helped Elena to a chair. She drank a little of the brandy in small sips. I felt bad being the bearer of the news and offered to help out in the kitchen, for Elena to have a rest. She thanked me for visiting Tobias and refused my offer. The two boys hurried about the business of meal preparation. Life went on in the Samaras house.

Between crying, cooking and plating up food, Elena sobbed out Tobias' story.

He wasn't a son, but Elena thought of him as one. She recalled a skinny, scruffy boy of about fifteen at the time ten years previously calling at the reception desk looking for work. He'd made his way down from the port village of Damarus. His father was a fisherman who'd been lost at sea, his mother destitute and unable to support them both. Elena was doubtful, Tobias seemed too frail for hard work, but she gave him a meal, a bath and a trial run for a day and never looked back. Tobias was a good worker, learned quickly, was polite and pleasant, good humoured and bonded well with Elena's two sons.

Dave Barton wasn't the first to give Tobias a hard time. In ten years never a season went by without some difficult guest giving him lip. But Tobias was a true professional and never complained nor retaliated. Barton was by far the worst guest ever. But still, Tobias never complained.

I suggested to Elena that if she was called as a character witness when Tobias went to trial that maybe she shouldn't mention the ill-treatment he'd received from certain guests. Like a trap, the prosecuting attorney would cite that as Tobias reaching his 'breaking point' over ten years of abuse. His best defence would be that no professional hotel worker would plot to murder a guest after only three days of bad-mouthing. If only I could tell that one to a lawyer. If Tobias even had one yet. I could still find out with another prison visit, but I thought I'd ridden my luck with Castellanos so far. If he turned up at the Courthouse again I wouldn't be able to help my sarcasm.

I retreated into Gouvia and Niko's Tavern for another beer before the evening meal to settle the day and my mind. Across the road the concert stage being erected last time I sat outside Niko's had been completed. Rows of bleachers had been set out in semicircles right up to the tall speakers each side of the stage. Men were busy pinning banners over the stage, and on stakes at each side of it. Another long banner was strung between two pine trees by the roadside as a makeshift entrance. The banners were written in Greek and I gathered it was a free affair from one of the few words in English lettering on one of them that seemed vaguely familiar: socialismós. Niko had told me two days before it was for a political rally. Now I guessed for which side. You didn't need to know Greek.

I had a quick one and was back at the Aeres early. I took up my place at a table in a quiet corner of the dining room, hoping to eat and be out before it got busy. Madge and Mabel had the same idea. They pulled chairs up as Christos served the first course of omelette, two inches thick, layered with green and red vegetables, cut into squares and looking like cake. I asked if it was cake. No, it wasn't cake. One day in the future chefs will disguise foods and surprise us all with an omelette that looks for all the world like a square of fruitcake. They only have to come to Gouvia to find out how.

The first course went down better than the bad news. 'I'm sorry, ladies,' I said. 'Castellanos found a phial in Tobias' room. It contained the same poison as was found in Barton's soup. We should keep it to ourselves for the time being. Elena's had about as much stress for the moment. Let her get over his arrest and not worsen things with spreading gossip all over the hotel. The problem with gossip is it starts small and idle and grows into a crisis within a short time. I don't want us to be the ones seen to have started it. All will become news in town soon enough. I'm sure Castellanos wants his fifteen minutes of fame as soon as he's squeezed a confession out of Tobias.'

'Oh, we won't say anything,' said Madge. 'It's such a shame, though. Poor Tobias, I can't believe he'd do such a thing. Can you believe that, Mabel?'

'I can't believe that,' said Mabel. 'It wouldn't surprise me if that horrible detective put it there himself.'

'I was thinking the same thing, Mabel,' said Madge. 'Maybe you could find out for us, Angelo?'

'I'll remind you both again,' I said. 'I'm not Jimmy Finn.'

'I know,' said Madge. 'But surely it must have crossed your mind. I mean what would Jimmy Finn do?'

'What *would* Jimmy Finn do...Angelo?' Mabel fluttered her eyelashes like two hungry Swallowtail butterflies descending on a cabbage patch.

'Right now he'd be asking for the main course then going for a beer or two.'

The main course came and went down moderately well. Pork chops, sauté potatoes and garden peas. Blancmange for desert. We stopped eating that back home in the 60s. But they did their best at the Aeres to get what they thought we wanted.

After the meal Jimmy Finn did what he said he would and took off into town for more beers. In the morning he asked Elena Samaras if there was somewhere quiet he could read and relax undisturbed. Somewhere he could perhaps do some writing. Half an hour later, while the rest of the guests had breakfast, he was on a sun-lounger napping with a newspaper over his face in the hotel's private garden with a glass of lemonade at his side made from lemons growing in the same garden and a notebook he had no intention of filling.

6.

The Aeres Hotel garden wasn't the quietest place on Earth. Beyond the hedge border of hibiscus and palm tree was the main road in and out of Gouvia. But the odd scooter and car didn't ask questions or ask if Jimmy Finn could investigate a crime in a foreign country. The garden itself led out from the kitchen into a large open space of orange, lemon and pomegranate trees, flower beds and vegetable plots whose produce found their way into our meals. They grew everything except blancmange and crème caramel.

I lay back on the lounger with my hat shading my forehead on the far side of the garden in a sunspot between the citrus trees, daydreaming and wondering what to do for the remainder of the day once Madge and Mabel had vacated and how was the best way of staying out of their way. The previous evening they'd said they were taking the bus to Paleokastritsa beach on the west coast for the day and invited me along. I said I'd think about it. In the morning, Elena led me out to the garden before they'd come down for breakfast. Paleokastritsa was a place I wanted to visit, just not today. And by myself.

I dozed and watched the Samaras family busy themselves through the open kitchen door. Somewhere in that non-awake, non-sleep space between kitchen chatter, scooter tutterings and misfires I imagined the hedge was talking to me.

It was.

A short way along the hedge line, Madge, in an emerald and red sarong, emerged like a brightly coloured bird from a hollow gap between a palm tree and hibiscus, stooping and holding her hat on against the branches. Mabel followed, in a green and yellow wrap, tugging at a denim beach bag caught behind.

'Ooh, good morning!' said Madge, trotting over as gingerly

as a cat called in for its breakfast. 'We thought it was you in here. We were just on our way to the bus stop for Paleokastritsa and we saw you through the leaves. We'd recognise that hat anywhere, so stylish it is. Exactly what a good crime writer should wear. And what a lovely garden! Isn't it a lovely garden, Mabel?'

'A lovely garden,' repeated Mabel. 'Oh, I wish our room overlooked the garden.'

It might as well, I thought.

'How did you get in here?' asked Madge. 'It's supposed to be private, you know. It says so in the dining room. You have to go through the kitchen to get in here, don't you?'

'The hedge works equally as well apparently,' I said. 'Actually, Mrs. Samaras let me in.'

'But why?' asked Madge.

I couldn't tell them the truth. As bothersome as they were and as much as I wanted some peace, they were still very nice ladies, a little lonely as individuals, perhaps, but they meant well. And Jimmy Finn was no snob. 'I'm on a stakeout,' I said. I lied. I couldn't tell them the truth – that I was avoiding them

'Ooh, fabulous!' said Madge.

'Fabulous!' repeated Mabel. 'Who are you looking for? Do you think someone else is about? Someone else who murdered Mr. Barton?'

'Where are you watching?' said Madge, looking about. 'Is that why you were pretending to be asleep? Are you watching through the hedge, watching the road for unusual activity? Jimmy Finn did a lot of that, watching roads for vehicles that didn't belong. Maybe we should leave, Mabel, we might blow his cover, or make him miss some unusual activity.'

'I'm watching the kitchen,' I quickly realised that my own words didn't make sense. Why would I watch the family? But now I had to play it.

'What are you watching the family for?' said Mabel. 'They

let you in the garden here, so even if you suspect it's one of them, they're not going to do anything unusual right in front of you, are they? Jimmy Finn wouldn't do anything so obvious.'

'No, silly,' said Madge. 'He must be waiting for that strange little man that comes around sometimes.'

'Strange little man,' said Mabel. 'He brings the produce, you know. The meat and fish from the Corfu market. We see him.'

I wasn't particularly interested. But I had to come up with a plot sometime to please the agent back home. I could probably start with some character creation for now. I sat up and swung my legs over the lounger and took a long drink of lemonade. 'He comes here?'

'Right into the kitchen,' said Madge. 'Shifty looking he is. He often calls when the family aren't even in the kitchen. They have an afternoon siesta, you know. They work such long hours and late and then get up early just for us tourists. Seven days a week all season they do that. Not something I could do, they're such hard workers.'

'Tell me more about this strange guy,' I said.

They described him comprehensively; right down to the colour of his red and black check socks he wore under sandals and the little two-stroke, three-wheeled flatbed wagon he delivered the meat and fish on. Other than his small stature and odd choice of foot attire there was nothing unusual, like many Greeks, olive skin, middle-aged and balding with a black moustache. And a lot of them drove two-stroke, three-wheeled flatbed wagons. One of them drove by and backfired on the other side of the hedge as Madge was speaking.

'I'll look out for him,' I said. I probably would, but probably wouldn't. It wasn't my business, but my curiosity was piqued. He might make a good character for my next book that I had no inclination to start yet. Jimmy Finn was on furlough and beer.

Madge and Mabel left then with apologies and hoped they hadn't disturbed my 'stakeout' and disappeared back through the hibiscus border. I lay back down, pulled my hat over my face and fell into a slumber to the music of Gouvia: kitchen chatter and clatter, chirping birds, badly tuned mopeds and two-stroke, three-wheeled flatbed wagons delivering groceries.

In the evening I felt guilty about deceiving Madge and Mabel, so I purchased two bottles of wine from the bar and took them to their table, a red Greek one and a white Greek one with no clue about grape variety, vintage or vineyard. They were written in Greek.

'Ooh, lovely!' said Mabel. 'What have we done to deserve this?'

'I suppose it's a thank you for not blabbing about my author identity or what detective Castellanos told me.'

'So how did the stakeout go?' Madge asked.

'The stakeout?' I said. 'Surely you realised it wasn't a real stakeout? I just wanted to position myself and imagine the comings and goings of anything or anyone suspicious. I was trying to get back into the writing groove. Sorry, I should have explained. I didn't see your shifty little man, by the way.'

'Oh, that's because he only comes on Mondays,' said Mabel. 'You were watching on the wrong day.'

'You never said anything.'

'Well,' said Madge, 'we wouldn't want to tell Jimmy Finn how to do his job, would we Mabel?'

'I'm not Jimmy Finn.'

'Of course not,' said Mabel. 'We just can't help thinking of you as Jimmy. We knew it wasn't a real stakeout, but we didn't want to say. We always imagined that Angelo Fox was the sort of crime writer that took inspiration from real life and we were right, there you were, pretending to sleep, but I bet that crime writing brain was buzzing with ideas, wasn't it?'

'Buzzing,' I said.

'So, do you really still think Tobias is guilty?' asked Madge.

'I'm afraid so. As much as I dislike detective Castellanos, I just can't think of any other likely suspect. There's no motive.'

Mabel looked deflated. 'Not even the little shifty looking delivery man?'

I poured out three glasses of the Greek red. 'It wouldn't suit him to do that. He'd be cutting his nose off to spite his face. If word gets out about the death he'll be losing the hotel's custom, his whole business even, if he became the main suspect. Look on the bright side, the soup is safe. Cheers.'

'It's such a shame, though,' said Madge. 'To think that poor Tobias could be driven to do something like that. And then there's all those other strange goings on in Gouvia.'

'What? What strange goings on?' I said.

'Well, Mr. Barton isn't the first, you know.'

'No, I don't know. What do you mean?'

'We heard that someone else dropped dead at the Alexander Hotel recently,' said Mabel. 'A younger one too, in their thirties they say.'

'And some others at the Orion,' said Madge. 'They were rushed to hospital with severe sickness and fainting.'

'Sounds like nothing more than food poisoning,' I said. 'It's not uncommon in a hot country.'

'And then there was the meat and fish lady,' said Mabel. 'Someone cut the power cables to the fridges in her shop one night. She lost all her stock.'

'Might explain the food poisoning,' I said.

'No, she had to destroy it all. Who on earth would do such a thing? The locals are blaming it on young drunk holidaymakers, but I doubt it could be them. Petty vandalism, maybe, but a deliberate act of sabotage?'

'And they would need to know about electrics,' said Madge. 'So they didn't electrocute themselves.'

'And there was that couple in the hire boat,' said Mabel. 'As soon as they were away from the shore it just blew up. Luckily the two weren't seriously injured and managed to swim to shore. I couldn't sleep that night. It did upset me so.'

'Mabel gets insomnia you know,' said Madge. 'Don't you dear?'

'Yes, alright Madge,' said Mabel. 'You've told him once already and I'm sure Angelo isn't interested. I admit it, but it's no big deal. I do have trouble with my nerves sometimes. But that's why we come here to relax. Life is at such a more pleasant pace. Or it was until all these recent events. It's so upsetting.'

'Well, perhaps this will help,' I said. One bottle down and I opened the white, pouring us all another round. I wasn't reading anything into their stories, but, against my will and the self-made promise to relax for the next few weeks, fiction town was forming in my mind along with a puzzling question. 'How the hell do you know all this?' I asked.

'We heard it,' said Mabel. 'It's all over Gouvia. Everyone's talking about it.'

'Well, I haven't heard anything.'

'Of course you won't hear it,' said Madge. 'That's because you don't speak Greek. The locals are talking about it all the time...in Greek of course. Obviously they don't want us tourists to hear in case we get nervous and don't come back. But we hear them talking all the time. Mabel speaks Greek you know.'

'I learned it at evening class,' said Mabel.

'Yes, I know, you said already,' I said.

'They're such lovely people and lovely language you know, especially that lovely waiter at Upsilon's bar. Dances to that Zorba the Greek song with a table in his mouth...'

'Wait...wait a minute,' I said. 'You heard all this in how long? Over how long? How long have you ladies been here in

Gouvia?'

'This time about four weeks. Is that about right, Madge?'

'Four weeks and a day,' replied Madge. 'Such a lovely place, Gouvia.'

'Lovely place,' repeated Mabel. 'Such a shame, though what's been going on.'

'All this happened in the last four weeks?' I asked.

'Yes,' said Madge. 'Very strange goings on, I must say.

'Very strange,' repeated Mabel.

I poured some more wine. Elena's eldest, Christos, brought side salads of tomato, cucumber and Greek feta to the table, then served minestrone soup from a hot tureen on a trolley. 'Tomato soup,' he said as he placed a basket of warm Greek bread rolls on the table.

'Bon appétit, ladies,' I said, sipping cautiously at the soup. 'How's the wine?'

'It's alright,' said Madge. 'There's not much choice at the hotel bar, is there? I'm afraid they assume the Brits drink beer all the time. But I have noticed that Jimmy Finn is a connoisseur of such fine things as wine in your novels, Angelo.'

I picked the nearly empty bottle of red up, pretending to read the label. 'Essences of Greek heather with a floral bouquet of two-stroke moped oil and a long finish of strychnine. Serve with unidentifiable soup and great caution.'

'That's not funny,' said Mabel.

7.

I took a long walk. I needed time away to think. No, I still didn't think Tobias was innocent, but a seed had been planted. Madge and Mabel's news had piqued my imagination and a story was brewing. Back home the agent would be expecting at least a synopsis from me when I returned. I knew he would phone me sometime, despite the cost of international calling. He'd make it brief. He was one of those things you have to learn to live with. Like herpes. You're fine most of the time but he'd come back into your life like an annoying itch. Maybe I'd give him one in another location? Jimmy Finn was a quiet, English village sleuth who was getting a bit bored of the quiet English village, middle and upper class gentry in their listed homes, Rolls and Bentleys the publisher insisted on. Fantasy Island stuff the publisher and agent said the readers wanted. I was never sure about this 'safe' option of filling a well-trodden genre of predictable mysteries for the sake of money. I always felt I was conning the reader into believing the English countryside was more dangerous than Beirut. Maybe the reader needed a three-wheeled, two-stroke flatbed wagon with a shifty looking little man in red and black check socks under sandals to stir things up. An idea was all I needed for now. I'd phone the agent, informing the fans that Jimmy Finn had a new case in a new location, a new tan and was solving crimes between moussaka and beer. Then I could forget about him and enjoy moussaka and beer.

So I stuck a notebook in the back pocket of my khakis and a pen in my sock and took off. From Gouvia bay I turned inland and found what passed for a coastal path north and hoping to get as far as Dassia beach where I could catch a bus back to Gouvia. Hard work and rough in places and disappearing in others, the path twisted in and out of woodlands and often led back to the beach where I had to stumble over rocks to find it again somewhere further up the coast which twisted around a couple of bays, then a short peninsula I cut across following around north again. But I was alone, just me and any idea for a story that might pop into mind. I met no one other than the odd local passing with burdened donkey, or shore fisherman casting nets. Then I could go no further. I was in a wooded area where no buildings were seen in any direction. The path turned down to a small sandy beach where a crowd of youngsters were partying. There was a campfire going and something barbecuing on a ring of sticks around it. I guessed they were from the Club 18-30 near the Aeres hotel from the stupid games. Kids were sat in two lines pretending to row boats to the tune of 'Oops, Upside Your Head' from a ghetto-blaster. Then the holiday rep would stop the music every so often and chuck a can of beer into the sea, at which the last two of each 'boat' would jump up at the cue and race each other to see who got it first. I don't think they needed any more beer. The last one I watched could barely stand. He couldn't swim either. Even if I wanted to walk past them, I could see that beyond the sandy beach, the coast stones had turned into small mountains. I was hungry and without the faintest notion of a synopsis and thirsty enough to swim for a beer. So I headed back to Gouvia on foot with no alternative but to retrace my route.

I needed to find that shifty-looking little man with a bald head, black moustache, black and red socks under sandals that drove a three-wheeled, two-stroke, flatbed little delivery truck. And there were a lot of those little trucks in Corfu. But only one that delivered to the Aeres every Monday.

He was right on schedule, just as Madge and Mabel had said, 2:00 PM Monday when the hotel was quiet. The Samaras

45

family had finished up the morning work, locked off the reception area, leaving hall access to the guests' rooms and disappeared for a well earned siesta before the chaos of evening meal preparation. I heard him coming, the tuttering of his little two-stroke truck as he turned into the hotel main entrance. I'd positioned myself across the road sat on a public bench with a good view pretending to read a newspaper. Just like Jimmy Finn would.

Nothing unusual ensued. He didn't look around or act shifty in any way. He unloaded his boxes off the back of the flatbed and disappeared inside. I followed, making my way past the reception to the dining room. I crept up to the kitchen swing door and pushed it open a crack, peering inside. His back was to me. Boxes of produce were stacked on the central work table and he appeared to be ticking off invoices. There was nothing unusual, not even the red and black check socks under sandals. In Gouvia that looked normal. He stacked the boxes in a walk-in fridge. Then came a surprise.

He went to the kitchen cabinets, opened one and took out plates and bowls, counting them. Maybe he was stock-checking? Maybe he also supplied hard stock to the hotels? He put them back and did the same for the cutlery drawers, counting every item and making a note.

I decided there was nothing to see here. Nothing more than the product of two elderly ladies imaginations. He was shifty looking, but that's all. Disappointed, I left him to it, no nearer to an idea for a synopsis. On the way out I took a photo of the little flatbed delivery truck for friends to laugh at back home. Right now I had a thirst and a mouth drier than a Mormon's wine cellar.

In the evening, over cream of oxtail cock-a-leekie, Greek wine, meatballs and red peppers stuffed with feta and olives (called florini) I put my observations to a disappointed Madge and Mabel.

'But why would he be counting plates and cutlery and rooting around in cupboards?' said Madge. 'It sounds very suspicious to me.'

'I think the likely reason is Elena's left him a note,' I said. 'Think about it, the family is far too busy to go running around shopping for plates. They'd probably have to go into Corfu Town for that. And I heard one break in the kitchen only last night. The guy must supply crockery as well.'

'Oh, well, that's disappointing,' said Madge. 'But didn't you go in after to see if Elena had actually left him a note? That's what Jimmy Finn would do.'

'What Jimmy Finn would do,' repeated Mabel.

'I'm not Jimmy Finn,' I said. 'And I'm not about to be caught by Elena or the boys snooping around in the family kitchen. The man had a legitimate reason to be there. I didn't.'

There was a long silence other than the pouring of wine, gentle dining chatter and clatter of knives in meatballs. Then I spoke: 'Look, I need to take off a while, tour a bit and see some of the island, maybe to relax my mind. The ideas just aren't coming yet. I think tomorrow I'm going to hop on a bus and take off north somewhere for the day. Maybe I'll visit Paleokastritsa, where you went.'

'Oh, you must!' said Madge. 'But why don't you hire a bike?'

'A bike?'

'A motorcycle, that's what Jimmy Finn would do.'

'I'm not Jimmy Finn.'

'He did do that,' said Mabel. 'He had a motorbike and used to tail suspects, didn't he? So he could pull into lay-bys unseen or go across the country trails to get ahead of the suspect, or hide behind the getaway house with his bike hidden in the woods. You couldn't do that in a car or on a bus, could you? You couldn't head them off at the pass.'

'I'm not the Lone Ranger.'

'But you must be careful,' said Madge. 'The roads can be very narrow and winding in Corfu. There were two lads from that Club 18-30 hotel down the road. They hired motorbikes and one of them drove right off the hillside road and landed in an olive tree. Their holiday rep came here and asked the Samaras boys to come and pull the bike back up the hillside with a rope attached to a Land Rover. They have a Land Rover, you know.'

'You're really selling this to me,' I said.

'But Jimmy Finn isn't some reckless teenager with no road sense,' said Madge.

'No, he isn't,' said Mabel.

'I'm not...oh forget it.'

So I hired a motorcycle.

8.

Motorcycle hire was popular in Gouvia. I got one of three remaining at the hire shop, a 100cc, two-stroke Suzuki that smoked like an Arbloth kipper hut, smelled the same and sounded like a sewing machine with worn bearings. The right footrest was higher than the left and the left handlebar was higher than the right, like it had been pulled out of an olive tree and dragged up a rocky hillside. It had a tendency to pull to the left if you didn't sit just right on the saddle. The hire guy assured me this was a good thing on Corfu roads.

I was away, carefree and nothing on my mind but a warm breeze through the remains of my hair and the buzz of a Singer Sew-o-Matic between my thighs. Born to be wild I was not. I had a pen, a pad and a packed lunch – thanks to Elena – in the rear pannier as I turned out of Gouvia onto the main road heading north to Paleokastritsa. There was a monastery there, Madge had said. I could get inspiration from the past history there, like the film Name of the Rose, or Cadfael, Mabel had said. Jimmy Finn doesn't do Monks, I'd said. It was another bright, beautiful day in Corfu in 1980. I was happy and didn't care that I'd forgotten to wear underpants or give a damn about monks, meatballs, friars, fried calamari, fava or florini. In the back of my mind Tobias was still hanging around along with detective Castellanos and a shifty-looking delivery man. Along with the mysterious deaths and an unexplained explosion, there were all the ingredients for a good mystery that just needed blending into some kind of coherent fiction. At odds with my agent, I'd come away wanting to forget about fiction, for a while at least, but recent events were too good an opportunity. I'd get the synopsis done today, no distractions, no small talk.

I didn't get there. I took a wrong turn somewhere before

Paleokastritsa and found myself on back roads near the west coast of the island. I didn't mind getting lost. The landscape was wilder, fresher, with less smell of restaurant and drains and more pine sap and wildflower. I stopped a while to take a drink, drink in the landscape and pulled out a map of the island, trying to figure out where I was. I didn't care, it was early and I'd find the way before evening. I had an urge to explore, so I kick-started the kipper smoker and set off again. Ahead of me, a vehicle pulled out of a side road, another one of those flatbed little trucks. I meant to pass, but then something struck me as an odd coincidence. I recognised the number plate from when I'd taken a photo outside the hotel. I was certain it was the same and the driver fitted, at least from behind he did. A little balding, black-haired man. With or without red and black check socks didn't matter, I was certain it was him. I slowed down, allowing him to gain speed, dropped back a little and followed from an unsuspicious distance. A mile or two on and he slowed down before a drive, stopped and got off the truck. I passed by slowly, catching sight of the gate. It looked to be solid timber, reinforced with riveted steel plate cross-sections, completely blanking off any view of what lay beyond and bookended by two posts with English-style carriage lamps on either side of the drive. There was a sign above the gate, but I didn't get a chance to read it. I didn't want to arouse suspicion in the little man by stopping and gawking at it. The property was fronted by a high stone wall either side of the gate. The wall was partly obscured by a pine tree border running its length, which was probably another hundred yards before it turned to woodland again. I pulled into the pines about half way along the wall, parked the bike up against a tree and sat waiting for the little man to come out again. I had a decent view of the drive entrance through the trees and doubted I'd be noticed in the shadows. Any passing vehicles and I was just another tourist stopping for lunch and siesta. So I had my lunch of sandwiches, tepid water and no siesta. I had the irresistible urge to follow him once he came out. So I waited and waited and waited. Three hours passed. I picked at the remains of Elena's revani cake I'd been saving for later. Another hour and no show.

Now I had a million questions I wanted to ask him then. Who lived inside the gate? What was he doing there? He wasn't simply delivering groceries. Even in Greece they don't take four hours to drop off groceries. And he wasn't any family member of any millionaire estate holder behind the gate. I couldn't wait any longer. I had a beer thirst and a motorcycle to return.

I rode slowly by the entrance and stopped. I took a few photos of the gate and its distinctive arched wrought iron name above. *Liontari Ilion*. There was something familiar about it – not the name, I had no clue what it meant – but the shape of it and how it curved in an elegant arc over the solid metal gate. The stone posts either side had cat-like figures carved into them and the one on the right had an intercom. I resisted the temptation to press it and ask if the visitor had red and black check socks.

Finding my way back to Gouvia, something else came to me and struck me as odd. I realised the little truck was already empty when he arrived at the gate.

He wasn't delivering anything.

In the evening I bought the wine again. I was pleased with the day's developments and felt a step nearer to a synopsis. I could make up any idea for why the shifty-looking little man went inside that fancy gate and never came out and it would make a good story, but I had more than a curiosity about it. I wanted to know why. As they say, truth is stranger than fiction. And more truth might lead to better fiction.

I poured three glasses of wine and wrote down on a slip of

paper the words I'd read on the sign over the gate and slid it across the table. Mabel took a cautious sip and beamed with delight. It was a decent, genuine Corfu white. One that didn't taste like pine trees or smell like turpentine. I'd purchased it on Madge's advice from a shop in Gouvia run by a lady who had no idea what I was saying and I had no idea what she was saying other than the magic words 'wine and Madge' and the language became universally understood.

'Liontari Ilion. It means Sun Lion,' said Mabel. 'And this is a rather good wine.'

'The Greeks usually try to keep it secret for themselves and sell us Brits the inferior stuff,' said Madge. 'No offence, Angelo, but that you bought last time wasn't so great, but you weren't to know.'

'None taken,' I said. 'I can see you've been around here a while. I wouldn't know one wine from the next. So what do you think of the sign? Could it possibly mean it's a zoo?' I mentioned the catlike carvings on the gateposts.

'That might explain the man not coming out,' said Madge. 'Maybe he's working part time as a zoo worker. Didn't you get a look inside the gate? Were there any buildings?'

'None I could see. The walls were too high and I could see trees beyond. Any buildings would be set back well away from the gate. I didn't actually see him go in from where I was watching, but he went in alright. There was no other way to go, either in there or back out on the road.'

'You must watch him some more, then,' said Madge. 'That's what Jimmy Finn would do.'

Mabel glanced at both Madge and I and said nothing. A forkful of omelette she held hovering near to mouth won out as I poured more wine.

I watched him some more. Before he'd disappeared inside that strange gate I'd lost all interest in him. But the shifty-

52

looking little man who did, whose business was supposed to be in grocery and hardware delivery was presenting more than a story. And whether innocent or other, I wanted to know it.

Keeping a tab on someone in Gouvia in 1980 wasn't hard. It's a small place and anyone could tail anyone on foot as long as the person you were tailing had business there and wasn't eager to be passing through. There was one main road, about 600 metres long and if you started at either end, walked a few minutes you'd have seen most of it. So I followed. Monday and he was right on time again at the Aeres, dropping off boxes of produce. It may or may not have been his first call, but it wasn't his last one in Gouvia. I walked briskly behind as he turned out of the hotel drive, watching and taking note of his drop-offs. Nothing unusual. I wandered in after him at one hotel, pretending to be a lost tourist. He didn't act too surprised, spoke reasonable English and was polite and explained that this was not the Hellas Bar and Hotel and pointed in the direction of it. He seemed less shifty up close, so I spoke a while, keeping it at friendly level, asking him how his business was going, if he served all the hotels and did he cater for restaurants as well. He did all that, he said, as he laid out and counted crockery on a worktop. I asked him about that. He supplied anything the hotelier or restaurateur wanted. He was amicable for sure. I asked him if he delivered to places out of the towns and villages, private residents or maybe even millionaires. He didn't, he said. I wanted him to say something about *Liontari Ilion*. He didn't so I said it for him.

'Beautiful weather we're having, wouldn't you say?' I said.

'Yes, summer is always good on Corfu, very hot.'

'The sun here is so hot it roars like a lion.'

It was like I'd swiped the plate from his hand myself. Onto the kitchen floor it crashed. He got down quickly, picking up the pieces. Then he stared up at me, a strange startled giveaway gleam in his eyes, but he said nothing.

'I can see you're busy,' I said. 'Sorry to disturb you.'

He made no reply and I left.

I waited until he emerged from the hotel and watched him a while from the other side of the road. I mingled in with the tourists on a shop boardwalk, pretending to be interested in rubber float rings, cheap sunglasses and flowery kaftans. He tut-tutted his little truck off down the road and took the next left down the lane leading to the boat hire wharf. Interesting.

He was hiding something, I knew that. But tailing him wasn't going to get me any nearer the truth. I had to get inside the Liontari Ilion, whatever it was.

9.

Madge recommended a holiday rep for more information. The same one that begged the Samaras boys for a Land Rover and tow rope to rescue two young idiots and a Suzuki from an olive tree. Apparently he'd worked on the island a number of years and knew a lot about it. Apparently the same one I'd seen chucking full beer cans into the sea and playing 'Oops, Upside Your Head,' for a bunch of kids. But Madge and Mabel insisted he was rather knowledgeable about the island and far more clever than his job title suggested. Apparently they'd cornered him after the bike rescue and kept him talking a while and taking photos for an afternoon. I'm sure he had fun. Madge said so and Mabel agreed.

He was more intelligent than I thought and more intelligent than he looked. He was definitely more intelligent than the kids he catered for. He had a degree in ancient history that impressed the tour company so much they gave him the lifestyle the university had promised, decent money, exotic travel and looking after ancient relics on Saga holidays as a bingo caller. He quit that for the new 18-30 Club and considered it a promotion. Maybe he wasn't that clever. Three years of hard study, one day of learning the top ten and one minute learning how to chuck full beer cans into the sea. And his name was Kevin.

Kevin was there every day at the Club 18-30, organizing stupid games and drunken tours to quiet villages. It used to be a respectable hotel called The Odyssey at one time I was told until the new, youngster catered for Holiday Company, renamed it Club 18-30 and stuck a huge obnoxious sign over the old one announcing it for anyone who couldn't find their way there following the racket and trail of vomit on the roadside.

I met Kevin at the Club's reception desk Saturday morning, a spotty faced blond, lightly tanned, big-toothed square steel glasses kid who'd never seen the Oxy 10 advert. I introduced myself and the kid gave his commiserations for the death at the Aeres. He still thought Barton died of heart attack or that's what the holiday firm had scripted him. And would I like to book a bouzouki night out while talking about the Liontari Ilion mansion? Mansion? I didn't know there was a mansion. And no, I didn't want to go on a bouzouki night and can you tell me a little about the Liontari Ilion mansion?

To my surprise, Kevin knew something about it. It was indeed the grounds to a mansion owned by one Hector Thanos, a wealthy property developer. The place was a former wartime hospital for Greek patriots and British troops. After the war Hector Thanos had purchased the disused property and converted it into his palace. Apparently he'd invested in community projects as well, community buildings, public spaces and parks. But Thanos was a recluse and was rarely seen. Kevin had heard rumours that he might be mafia or some head of gangland mobsters. I'd be best advised to keep away. All the more reason for me to pay a visit. I needed to know more. A synopsis was brewing.

Property developer. It gave me an idea, or rather an excuse to come calling. But in the meantime another problem arose. Word had got out about how Dave Barton had died and it didn't come from Madge or Mabel. A British tabloid newspaper had put a small article about a Brit being poisoned in a hotel and the news spread like wildfire between tourists. The residents of the Aeres didn't like it. Some accused Elena Samaras of keeping the truth from them and some demanded the holiday company move them to other hotels in the area.

Within a couple of days the Aeres was half empty and Elena was heartbroken. Madge, Mabel and I stayed loyal. We worked out two axioms that we couldn't convince the Aeres residents with. One was that the poisoner was in prison; the other was that if he wasn't in prison and Tobias was innocent, then the real poisoner was still out and about and could still strike at any other hotel they chose to move to. Some people are still thick.

It was time for me to pay a call on a property developer recluse. I needed a car for this one. If I was going to call in on a property developer pretending to be a property investor, I needed to look at least professional. I could hardly arrive on a vehicle that looked like it had been dragged out of an olive tree. I got a car whose make I'd never heard of before, a Seat. Maybe because it had seats. It reminded me of those cramped little Pandas we had back home with floor pedals so close you could stamp on your own left foot when braking. It would do. Even a millionaire would know a Brit tourist couldn't hire a Mercedes in Gouvia. I changed into light slacks and suede tan loafers, light blue shirt and tan jacket. For an added touch I put a folded white hanky in the lapel pocket and wore a white suede trilby that hadn't been face sweated into trying to hide from two elderly ladies. Finally I grabbed my compact Kodak Ektra that so far had only photos of me with Madge and Mabel that they insisted would provide me with fond memories of our time together in Gouvia. I slipped it into my left pocket. By noon I was away, heading for the west coast, making less smoke but no more comfortable than a Suzuki with odd handlebars.

10.

The trip lasted longer than I'd anticipated. I missed the wrong turnoff I'd taken previously, which should have been the right turnoff this time around and found myself nearly in Paleokastritsa before realizing my mistake. It's what happens when you're not paying attention and thinking only of how you're going to bluff it to a millionaire property developer you've never met before.

It was still early afternoon when I arrived at the big gate. I was glad to get out of my Seat and stretch, brush off some of the road dust gathered through open windows on another uncomfortably warm day. I took my jacket off, shook it out, put it back on, straightened my shirt collar and pressed the intercom.

It seemed ages but was probably only half a minute of nervous anticipation before the speaker crackled into life.

'*Geia sas, pos mporo nha sas boetheso?*'

'Hello, I'm sorry to disturb you. Do you speak English?'

'*Yes.*' The reply came after a short silence. '*I speak English. Can I help you? Are you lost?*'

'No, sir, I am not lost. I understand you are a property developer. I am interested in purchasing some property here on Corfu and was told you are something of an expert in the field.'

'*Who are you?*'

'My name is Angelo Fox. I am a writer and am looking to establish a writer's retreat here. Somewhere quiet. Somewhere a man can get peace of mind and inspiration.'

'*You are from Britain?*'

'Yes.'

There was another uncomfortable silence. I was half expecting to be told to get lost when a loud click came from the gate and slowly it creaked open. The wrought iron sign above divided into *Liontari* and *Ilion* on either side.

It was a mansion, alright, done out in the Greek revival style. Whatever it had looked like as a wartime hospital, I doubted this was it. It was fronted by six huge marble-like columns, three each side of a raised portico, high enough to get a real good view of all the stinking wealth that led to it below. There were three sets of stairs, one each side of the portico behind the columns and the main set at the front, all leading to a red, solid wood arched double door high enough for a basketball team. It was brick built – something I hadn't seen on Corfu so far – with white stone corners that made it as elegant as a wedding cake. The main drive to the stairs was paved mosaics of reds, greens and blues of Byzantine style depicting Gods or myths or battles of some sort. I didn't want to drive on it, even though I could see a black shiny big European car parked in front of the right-hand columns. I wasn't going to park my crappy hire car next to it. Oil might leak on the mosaic. I left it outside the gate and walked the drive, about fifty yards or so to the entrance between prim lawns, sculpted topiary and flower beds overflowing with colours that echoed the mosaics. The place stunk of wealth, but it was a nice smell. I like that smell, maybe one day I'd stink of it myself. I glanced round as the gate creaked closed behind, wondering if there was another way out. I carried on.

The front door opened before I had chance to swing the knocker. I was expecting some kind of butler or manservant, elegantly attired to greet me. I got a sixty-something looking guy in grey shorts, white short-sleeved Oxford-style shirt and Dunlop trainers. He looked a hard case. He was taller than me and muscular. I could tell he was solid-jawed under the neatly styled grey Van Dyke beard. He had a head of fine grey hair, crew-cut style and grey-blue eyes. I thought I detected a scar under the beard.

He held a hand out and we shook. 'Pleased to meet you, Mr. Fox,' he said. 'I am Hector Thanos and this is my home. Won't you come in?'

'Thank you for having me.'

He led me in. He walked with a gait that looked like someone had kicked him hard sometime. I wouldn't envy the guy who tried it. We went into an extensive whitewashed entrance hall with a huge crystal chandelier that probably had more lights than Gouvia and one of those grandiose central curved white staircases you expect Fred Astaire and Ginger Rogers to come tap dancing and banister sliding down with a load of showgirls. Huge glazed pots of plants were everywhere. A grand piano stood on mosaic flooring in the middle of the entrance hall. It was cooler inside, but I could see no air conditioning system. Maybe that's just how mansions were designed.

Thanos looked me up and down. 'You must be thirsty? You English amuse me, the way you always overdress for the weather. Out here you have no one to impress. May I offer you a drink of something long and cool? And please remove your jacket. You are making me feel warm just looking at you.'

I didn't need asking twice. He took my jacket and hat and led me through a high door to the left of the hall, into another reception room and down some stairs into a large rustic kitchen. Three large British made Aga cookers and sinks lined one wall; high handmade solid wood cupboards the other. Herbs and pewter tankards hung from dark wood beams above a long, thick wooden central table.

'It's always a little cooler down here when stoves are off.' said Thanos. 'The cook left some time ago. I once had staff here, but when my wife deserted me I felt no need anymore.'

'I'm sorry to hear that,' I said.

'There is no need, Mr. Fox. I am not alone. I have my best friend Charlie.'

'Charlie?'

'I'll introduce you later. In the meantime, that long drink I promised.'

He invited me to sit at one of the stools around the central table and opened one of three fridges big enough to park a Seat in and brought a large earthenware jug to the table. He poured out two long glasses.

'Lemonade,' he said. 'I made this myself, fresh from the orchard. It has some spices, a little ginger and other botanicals that are good for longevity. And there is a little fermentation. Good health, as the English say. Is good, no?'

I took a cautious sip. It seemed safe. It was also delicious. 'Excellent. It's very refreshing.'

'But we are not here to talk about lemonade,' said Thanos. 'Perhaps I can show you around and tell you a little about Liontari Ilion while we discuss your interests in property investment?'

'Thank you, that's most kind,' I said.

We finished our drinks and Thanos led me back to the entrance hall. I asked him if he ever considered getting Mark Sandrich to film a musical here.

He laughed at that and knew what I meant. 'The staircase you mean? Indeed, it would be quite suitable. I can tell you are a writer, Mr. Fox, you have a good imagination. This staircase did not exist when I purchased the property, nor did the entire upstairs floor. These I had built from my own designs. All that remains of the old hospital is the ground floor. Behind the staircase is the old ward, very large but completely unrecognisable now. So much investment and hard work.'

Thanos invited me to follow and we ascended to a long landing guarded by white balusters. The place seemed to be all whitewashed plaster without ceiling cornices. The floor was glazed mosaic in classic Greek design with birds and plants among regular patterns. Two halls to either side led to the bedrooms, Thanos explained, eight in all. He didn't show me them and I was disappointed. I didn't want the estate agent speech, but I wanted to know what was in them. Instead he lead the way up another flight and out through a door leading onto the rooftop. There was a full length, white balustrade at the front of the house. From there I could see the sea, the wilder and largely unoccupied west coast of the island.

'So you are here to talk about property,' said Thanos. 'I can help you. I know the best places that are for sale. Perhaps I could interest you in one of my own? I have a wide portfolio. You see, Mr. Fox, I am pleased that you have come here today.'

'Really? Why?'

'Corfu needs more people like you. At one time Mr. Fox, the visitors to Corfu were like you. There were writers and artists and professional people that would come to enjoy our island and its beauty. Many years ago they would come and find the very solace and inspiration that you yourself seek. You are looking for a writer's retreat? That is an excellent ambition.'

I nodded my head in agreement. The lie was working. I still wasn't relaxing. I had neither the money nor inclination to establish a writer's retreat on Corfu or Timbuktu. Jimmy Finn was a loner, same as his creator. And Thanos had an accent that was Greek, but not quite. His Greek accent was off-Greek and that made me uneasy.

'But what do we have now?' said Thanos.

'I don't know. What do you mean?'

'I will tell you what we have, Mr. Fox. We have a new type of tourist here. A tourist that has no respect for Corfu. Young people with too much money and too much time on their hands. Drunken party people that defile our streets and beaches. Young women who are equal as vandals as their male counterparts, showing too much flesh and acting like whores.

They litter everywhere, drink too much and throw up and urinate in the streets. They have no respect for us here, our ways and traditions. You think they come here to admire our culture, our way of life, our art and history? No. They come here to get drunk and be sick everywhere. And you know what?'

'No...what?'

'The hoteliers turn a blind eye and pretend it doesn't matter. Why? Because they are making more money than they ever have before from these hooligans. And now, as a final insult, we are invaded by this 'organised hooliganism,' this latest scab on our lives called the Club 18-30. Not only are these hooligans coming here to disrespect our way of life, but now they have an entire business that organises these drunken parties and beach debauchery.'

Now was not a good time for him to ask who recommended him to me. I hadn't prepared an alternative person for Kevin the Club 18-30 DJ and beer can chucker.

'So, Mr. Fox, I welcome you and your new suggestion for investment here. I want more people like you to come to Corfu. I would love to turn the clock back to a better time, to when the people with souls and creative spirit came. You, Mr. Fox, are a godsend. Perhaps once you establish your retreat, others will follow, replacing this cancer in our villages. That is my dream, that one day the scum tourist will be replaced by good people.'

We took a walk to the back and viewed the property from the rear balustrade. There was a huge garden, maybe the length of a football pitch, of citrus orchard, prim lawns, olive trees and winding mosaic paths bordered with pine. Every scent of the Ionian seemed to drift in along the breeze from up there. All of it was in a deep enclosed rectangle wall in that same stone that extended from around the front. I estimated it about twenty feet high and the same width as the front road face. Beyond that was forest and hills. I couldn't see another house or building. Thanos truly was a recluse.

He invited me back downstairs. We passed a lot of doors, none of them open and came to a study overlooking the lawns and orchard. It was also whitewash, with a large brick fireplace and an oak table by a huge bay with four sash windows, more plants in colourful glazed pots, a large bureau and lots of empty space. Over the fireplace was an empty place where you'd expect a painting or mirror. I'd noticed this in the reception area too and on the upstairs landing. There was a lot of empty space, but no dirty marks like any pictures had been taken down.

'What happened to the picture?' I asked. I stared at the chimney breast like it was Rauschenberg painting. The ones that aren't paintings, just blank canvas.

'I have no pictures,' said Thanos. 'That would affect my original vision for this house. It's called Minimalism. The house itself is the art.'

'I see.' I didn't see. I knew Minimalism didn't mean a lot of huge plants in giant vases with oak tables or bureaus and fancy mosaic. A millionaire would have paintings. Thanos just wasn't showing his.

'But let us talk about property.' Thanos invited me to the bureau, unlocked the top doors and removed a series of filing cases to the table by the window. 'I suggest somewhere in the north of the island. It is quieter there.'

'Gouvia would do for me,' I said. 'Sometimes things can be a little too quiet. People inspire me. Sometimes I want to be around people, for ideas, you see? It's called characterisation. I create fictional characters, but I get the ideas for them from real people, if that makes sense.'

'But of course. It makes perfect sense, Mr. Fox. Gouvia is a beautiful village. But it also seems to have been fouled by this new tourist invasion of the uncouth. Perhaps if I can secure you a premise there, on the outskirts of the village where it's quieter, then others may follow. Maybe we can once again have a place of tranquil beauty unspoilt by these rogues.'

'That's not really what I meant. Some of my best friends are rogues.'

Thanos looked at me strangely. Then he laughed. 'Very good, Mr. Fox. I can tell you are a writer, you have such an insight into humanity, yet you take no bull, as they say. Everybody has a rogue friend somewhere, but you are so blasé and unconcerned like nothing bothers you. But please, have a look at some properties.'

He emptied a filing case out onto the table and spread out papers of ordinance maps, building layout plans, property photos of both exterior and interiors. Some were hotels, some were empty plots. Thanos selected some images and sale notices of Gouvia properties and slid them over. I leafed through some, pretending to be interested.

Something pushed my left leg from behind.

Thanos turned around. 'Aha, Charlie, there you are!'

I turned, reaching my hand down instinctively at the dog pushing against me and promptly jumped away. It was no dog. It was a cat and a big one.

A Cheetah.

I backed away around to the window side of the table, looking for an opening. The sash windows were shut. I noticed the thumb-swivel locks weren't on, but I had no chance of opening one in time, even if a sash window did open first time like they rarely do without a struggle. It didn't matter anyway. Nothing was going to get past this security guard. It was following me, sniffing the air I'd left and I'd left some alright.

'Do not be alarmed, Mr. Fox. Charlie is so gentle, aren't you Charlie?' Thanos bent forward, slapping his thighs and the cheetah lost interest in me, trotting over to Thanos enthusiastically, reaching up on its hind legs and nuzzling

Thanos' neck. It purred like a house cat, but loud like distant thunder as it licked Thanos' neck and ears.

'Forgive me, Mr. Fox, perhaps I should have told you.'

'Damn right you should. Have you got a licence for this thing?'

'But of course. I have had Charlie from a cub. He's so house trained and very friendly. He won't hurt you, Mr. Fox. Please, come and say hello.'

Thanos played with it. It rolled on the floor just like any housecat as Thanos ruffled its spotted coat and stroked its black tear-marked muzzle. Its eyes, amber like two gemstones, watched me as it played.

'I'm fine right here, thanks,' I said. 'Maybe finer if I just leave now.'

'Charlie is fine with people, Mr. Fox. Others have made his acquaintance and are quite at ease.'

'Maybe,' I said. 'He hasn't known me since kittenhood, though.'

'Cub is the correct term for a young cheetah, Mr. Fox, as are most big cats. Housecats are called kittens.'

Charlie got up, sniffing and purring. It crept under the table towards me, rubbing its handsome face and flank against the table legs as it went. It was no good running or jumping on the table. Thanos wouldn't thank me for damaging what may well have been a Chippendale piece and if the beast really wanted to catch me it would. So I stood there like a snowman and let it nuzzle my legs and sniff my lower quarters. I dared to reach my hand out and like any cat it rose to greet it, pushing its face sideways against it. I didn't stroke it, it stroked me. I felt a little more comfortable. I'd also read somewhere that cat purring can also indicate hunger and stress, so I wasn't that comfortable. I was just there with a big carnivore and couldn't do a damn thing about it.

'Well done, Mr. Fox,' said Thanos. 'Charlie likes you and

you now have a new friend.'

'I wouldn't like to meet your enemies. You got any more friends I haven't met?'

Thanos laughed. 'No, Mr. Fox, only Charlie. But please, we have business. I will take care of Charlie.'

'Wait,' I said. 'You mind if I take a picture? This would be some memo. 'How about if I get you and Charlie in the frame?'

I wanted more than a memo, although I didn't know exactly what I was looking for. I wanted to know the real reason for having a big cat. I wanted to know why the shifty flatbed driver had been here if he wasn't delivering groceries. I wanted a photo of Thanos, but I wasn't sure why. He was a successful businessman and seemed a nice guy. Most of them are on the surface. Maybe Kevin was right.

'No...no, Mr. Fox,' said Thanos. 'I am not very photogenic. But please, you may take one of Charlie, perhaps one of you and Charlie together, to show your friends your new friend?'

Charlie slipped back under the table. I took out my Ektra, came round the table and took a couple of snaps of Charlie rolling on the floor.

'I'll take up your offer,' I said. 'One of me with Charlie.' I handed him the camera.

'A very nice device,' said Thanos. I showed him how to slide the lens protecting handle out and down, explaining the steadying qualities of having a full hand grip.

I knelt down next to Charlie, carefully stroking his neck. 'Where do you keep him? You got a cage or outdoor pen for him?'

'Charlie is a free agent. It would be wrong to keep him locked up. He lives primarily outside. It is sad sometimes. I believe Charlie pines for a mate, but to introduce one might bring out aggression in him. It is not worth the risk. I hear him sometimes, such as when the moon is full. He barks out a mating call and listens for a reply that never comes. Then he gives up after a while and one can hear a gentle chirp, rather like the sound of a child crying in the distance.'

'Is that safe to let him wander about by himself outside? What if he climbs out?'

'Ah, good question, Mr. Fox. But cheetahs are not good climbers. Unlike other cats, they don't have retractable claws. They are static, rather like a dog's claw. A cheetah's paws are designed for speed. He may climb a tree if the branches are low enough, or the tree is bowed, but Charlie could never scale the walls here, so he is quite safe.'

'Not like anyone who decided to break in, eh?'

'Precisely. Charlie would be unlikely to harm an intruder, but anyone coming face to face with him would surely vacate very quickly.'

Thanos held the camera up and clicked it as I stroked Charlie. 'Hmm,' he said. 'I can't seem to find the viewfinder.'

'Wrong way around,' I said. I got up and showed him, then knelt back down with Charlie. 'You must be left-handed.'

Thanos made no reply and took a couple of photos and handed back the camera. 'We should talk more business. Excuse me for the moment. I must take care of Charlie first.' He disappeared with Charlie trotting behind enthusiastically with his tail in the air, leaving me to inspect the properties. I was only interested in his and took a few more snaps.

A squeal came from the window. Outside on the lawn a small pig, probably barely out of suckling stage, was running between the trees without direction. It was distressed. It screamed like a child, a shrill and terrified cry. Charlie appeared out of nowhere and shot across the lawn, skidded onto his side on the mosaic path, spun and landed back on his feet without stopping or losing speed. He crashed into the pig sending it into the air as he skidded again, or did the pig jump? It was difficult to tell in that split second of contact. Charlie regained his feet and leapt before the spinning pig had chance to land. It all happened in a couple of seconds. Charlie snatched the pig by the hindquarter in his jaws midflight and landed rolling and sliding to a stop. He lay there on the lawn panting, his two front paws holding the struggling and screaming pig down. The pig escaped, making a futile attempt to run, its hind leg crippled from Charlie's bite. Charlie watched the pig a while as it tried to drag itself forward by its front legs, leaving a smear of blood on the grass before he pounced again, swatting it like a house cat swats a mouse. He picked the pig up by the throat and threw it in the air. When it landed he watched the pig until it stopped squealing. It lay quivering in shock. Then he began to tear strips off it, chewing and twisting his head side to side at each mouthful just like a cat chews a live mouse. I imagine it was purring again. I was transfixed, not horrified or sickened. I'd seen enough wildlife documentaries to realise this was life playing out before me, shocking yet sublime.

So transfixed I didn't notice Thanos was back in the room. He stood next to me, making me jump when he spoke. 'Such a beautiful display of prowess, wouldn't you agree, Mr. Fox?'

'I suppose. Is this legal? Sort of unfair on the pig, isn't it? Can't you just throw him a big chunk of meat for lunch?'

'Of course it's legal. We are on Greek laws here, not under the strains of such animal rights groups as you have in Britain. This is no more cruel than a slaughter house and far more sanitary. As soon as Charlie strikes, the pig goes into shock, it feels nothing and dies quickly and Charlie devours it just as quickly. Cheetahs are not scavengers, they will not eat remains they did not kill themselves. Unlike other African predators, lions, hyenas, and even vultures will drive a cheetah away from its kill, so it is in a cheetah's instinct to eat quickly or flee to avoid confrontations. Watch and observe again, Mr. Fox.'

Charlie ripped another strip out of the carcass, chewed a few seconds, then picked the pig up and disappeared behind a grove of lemons.

'See what I mean, Mr. Fox? Even though there is no competition for his kill here, it's in Charlie's genetics, inbuilt that's telling him he must hide away with his prize, even though he's never met a hyena or lion in his lifetime. It's evolution, clever genes of a true survivor and hunter. You see, Mr. Fox, there are in this world survivors and hunters in all the animal kingdom, even the human race. Especially in the human race. We today are the product of survival of the fittest, as your own Mr. Darwin once said.'

'Sure,' I said. 'I'd still just give him a piece of meat.'

'That, Mr. Fox, is exactly what is wrong in this world today.'

'I'm not with you?'

'There are those that contribute and those that just take and assume it is their God-given right not to give something in return. On the one hand there are those that are just 'given a piece of meat' as you say, without earning it. Then there are the hard workers, the selfless people that do everything to bring up decent families with respect for the law and their fellow man. And people like yourself, Mr. Fox. The creators, the artists who write and make beautiful things that give so much joy and culture to the world, making it a better place for all. For all that appreciate it, that is. And there are those that have no concept of art, work ethic, dignity or culture. It is as if Darwin's ideal of humanity as the ultimate development of evolution was a waste. That waste is here amongst us. Those that have not earned a place on this earth, that don't deserve to be here. These rogues, as you call them. They are the waste product of evolution, the useless consumers that we all pay for and get nothing in return. If there was an apocalyptic event tomorrow, who do you think would survive it, Mr. Fox?'

'You and Charlie, for sure.'

Thanos stared at me, a long cold sideways stare that nipped

my ears like a frost. He broke into a slow smile that felt like an hour but was only a few seconds. 'The strongest, Mr. Fox. Charlie, yes, he would hunt and kill whatever lived after. Also the articulate, the creators that use their intuition; that is the survival of the fittest. That is how it should be in an ideal world, reward for those that contribute, annihilation for those that don't. That is why I'm so happy you have come to me, Mr. Fox.'

'You want me to annihilate a few people?'

Thanos gave me another stare, a shorter one this time. He laughed. 'Your writers retreat will be just the start, Mr. Fox. Corfu will once again be a place for beautiful people.'

Charlie appeared shortly from behind the trees. He flopped on the mosaic path in the sun and licked his bloody paws and lips. He looked up briefly at us observing him through the window.

'He could do that to me, couldn't he?' I said.

'If he so desired,' said Thanos. 'But Charlie has never known other cheetahs. He sees humans as his own kind, so would never attack. But I am forgetting my manners. You must be hungry. Would you like to stay for tea, Mr. Fox, while we discuss some more properties and your ideas for a retreat?'

'Will I have to run after it in the garden?'

'I can tell you are a creative, Mr. Fox. Such a sense of humour. But I have English crumpets in the freezer and jam and real Twinings English tea, should you wish to stay.'

'It's a nice offer, but I really should go. There's two nice ladies at the Aeres and it's their turn to bring wine for the evening meal. I can hardly leave two ladies alone with extra wine.'

'Two ladies?' Thanos smiled and his eyebrows raised. 'That does not surprise me, Mr. Fox. Such a charming man you are and so intelligent. I assume you are unattached?'

'It's not like that,' I said. 'They're quite elderly and

charming in their own quirky way and I made a promise.'

'Of course. A lady should never be kept waiting, never mind two ladies. Another time for tea then perhaps, Mr. Fox? I look forward to seeing you again, should you wish to know more about properties. Please, take the sheets with you and perhaps have a wander around to some of the locations, then come back at your leisure. Charlie and I welcome you.'

'As long as Charlie doesn't want me for tea, I'm fine.' I took another look at Charlie still sunning himself on the mosaics and cleaning his bloodied face with a licked paw before Thanos showed me out, returning my hat and jacket. We had a final handshake and I walked the beautiful path that stunk of wealth to the electric gate already opening halfway before I got to it.

It wasn't that late and I had plenty of time to get to the Aeres before mealtime. But I had to get away from Thanos for some breathing time before seeing Madge and Mabel – who would no doubt cloud my thinking with their own input – to figure out exactly what he was, or what he was up to; if he was an eccentric reclusive genius who'd invested a lot in the development and infrastructure of the island...or a nutcase.

11.

'He's a nutcase,' said Madge.

I poured three glasses of a nice red and we picked at black and green olives while awaiting the main meal. The dining room was subdued and half empty. Soft background music drifted from a portable tape player in the corner. This was new. I think it was Elena's attempt at calming the few guests that remained loyal and hadn't run like scared chickens to the holiday rep demanding a change of hotel.

'Tell me why you think so,' I said.

'Well, it's obvious, isn't it?' said Madge. 'So he wants to drive out the scum, like he thinks all young tourists are some kind of sub-human species. Doesn't he realise these so-called rogues are a huge part of the Greek economy?'

'He did allude to that. He blames the hoteliers as much for accepting them. To be honest, if the Aeres was full of youngsters, I think most of them would still be here. Kids these days live life like it's one big dare.'

'Well I think he's some extremist, just like that Enoch Powell, looking to blame one group or other for all the world's ills.'

'You haven't heard the half of it,' I said. 'He has a pet cheetah.'

'Oh, how lovely!' said Mabel. 'A pet monkey! A cheetah, like in the Tarzan films!'

Madge rolled her eyes and backhand slapped Mabel on the arm. 'Don't be ridiculous, Mabel. Cheetah was the *name* of the chimpanzee in Tarzan. Angelo's talking about a big cat, like the sort that could rip your heart out if it was hungry enough.'

'Oh dear,' said Mabel. 'That sounds rather frightening. I suppose it's alright though, as long as it's caged.'

'It isn't.' I said. 'It wanders about the place free as a

household tabby.' I explained the rest of it, the story Thanos gave me about raising it from a cub and the kill it made right in front of me out on Thanos' back lawn. 'In fact, it rather likes me. Just like a cat, it was friendly and liked to be stroked and was quite playful.'

'Oh, that's awful,' said Mabel. 'What a horrible thing to allow it to kill like that. He sounds like a horrible man.'

'This is sort of putting me off the meal,' said Madge. She dropped an olive back in its bowl and took a sip of wine.

'Speaking of which, I wonder what's on the menu tonight?' I caught Christos' attention as he passed. Moussaka, he told us.

'Greek food,' I said. 'Looks like I've poured the right wine. You think they'll get this one right, I mean it's their own national dish. It won't be steak and kidney pie, will it? If the soup list is anything to go by we could be having fish.'

'Oh do stop making light of it,' said Madge. 'I do believe you're doing this on purpose. In fact, I think you've made up the part about a cheetah. It's like when you were in the garden saying you were doing a stakeout. You were really just gathering ideas for your next book. That's what you're doing now, isn't it? You're letting your imagination run and not letting go of it until you've got your synopsis. I like the idea, though, a villain that has a wild carnivore to protect himself.' Madge reached across the table and patted my hand like a child who'd just shown his mummy a crap crayon drawing. 'It sounds like a fabulous story, Angelo. We can't wait to read it, can we, Mabel?'

'We can't wait,' repeated Mabel.

The moussaka came and it was moussaka. And it was quite good. Greeks try their best to accommodate us Brits and make us feel at home cuisine-wise, but they really excel at their home dishes. I decided to shut up a while and just enjoy the meal — which came with a basket of chips. It worked for me and the Angel Delight with a fine white for dessert wasn't too bad either.

'I can prove it,' I said. 'I can prove that Thanos has a real cheetah as a pet.'

'Oh, you're not still on about that, are you?' said Madge. 'I think you're just teasing us now.'

'Seriously, I have photos. I took some photos of it and Thanos took a couple of me playing with the cheetah. It's called Charlie, by the way.'

'Charlie the cheetah, indeed. Now I know you're taking the Mickey. I'll bet you can't prove it.'

'You're on,' I said. 'As soon as I get back to England I'll have them developed and send you the prints. How much do you want to bet?'

'Ha! You don't get off that easy,' said Madge. 'I'll wager you prove it and I'll buy the wine for the rest of our stay here. I want to see these so-called Charlie the cheetah photos now.'

'How? If I even find a developer here on the island it'll take at least a week for them to come back.'

'Tell him, Mabel.'

'We passed a camera and photo shop in Corfu Town not long after we arrived,' said Mabel. 'It said "twenty-four hour photos guaranteed." It was in plain English too. Your photos returned next day, it said. It must be especially for the tourists. They get impatient you know...some tourists.'

'That's got you,' said Madge.

'That's got you,' repeated Mabel. 'How is Jimmy Finn going to get out of this one then?'

'In the morning Jimmy Finn's off to town,' I said. 'And the evening of the following day he's drinking free wine.'

I still had the Seat for another couple of days, but decided to take the early bus into Corfu Town so I could take in a bar or two and finish off the film roll around the harbour and historic buildings and park before handing them in. I found the camera shop sure enough where Madge had said it was and indeed it was "twenty-four hour returns." The proprietor was an American starting a franchise in the business of quick photo processing in holiday resorts, like they already had in the States. He had his own lab, was free of outside contracting and was hoping to capitalise on the quick turnaround market in other European resorts. Business was good, he said. He pointed me in the direction of a wine shop owned by an ex-pat. I purchased my last ever bottles, six in all, at a multi-purchase discount store, of some expensive, highly recommended, unheard of grape variety, caught the afternoon bus to Gouvia and delighted Madge and Mabel with my purchase.

I came back the following day in the Seat, paid over the odds for the prints confident that it would more than balance out in free wine for our stay and headed back to the Aeres.

In the evening over another round of the pricey wine, I slid the photo envelope across the table to Madge. She flicked through them, placing each one on the table at a time. Two snaps of me and Charlie were laid out and Madge sighed. 'Looks like you've won,' she said. 'Although you hardly look to be playing with it, so I'm not sure that counts.'

'Oh don't be such a spoilsport!' said Mabel. 'Angelo's won fair and square. Anyway, we share everything on holiday, so I'll share the cost of the wine with you.'

'But look at him, Mabel.' Madge passed her the print. 'He looks terrified. That's not playing.'

Christos brought our soup course and we fell silent. Madge shuffled through the rest of the prints as she ate, then suddenly snorted and coughed and choked. She dropped her spoon, grabbed a napkin and coughed into it violently. All eyes in the dining room were on her. A ripple of chatter went through the guests. Spoons were dropped, into bowls and one onto the floor. I heard the word 'poison' whispered amongst the exchanges. Someone got up to come over. Madge ceased to cough, dropped the napkin and smiled, then laughed, a choking laugh, a chortle between coughs. Everyone breathed a sigh of relief. She held up one of the prints. It was Thanos. A close-up of his face.

'Why did you take one like this?' Madge was still cough/laughing.

'I didn't,' I said. 'I'd forgotten that happened. Thanos was holding the camera wrong way around. He'd never seen a Kodak Ektra and held it in his right. He's left-handed, I think. I meant to throw that one away.'

Madge passed the photo to Mabel. Mabel frowned, picked it up, looked at it at arm's length and then smiled. 'Oh, it does look a bit funny. He looks puzzled, like one of those criminals in a police mug shot, frowning like they can't understand how they got caught. But his face is so close it fills the photo! Don't throw it away, it's quite funny!'

'You can keep that one as long as the bet is honoured,' I said.

'Well, how could we possibly refuse?' said Madge. She raised her glass. 'Here's to Jimmy Finn and his next novel.'

'His next novel,' repeated Mabel. 'Looks like Angelo's outfoxed you this time, Madge.'

'That's rather clever, Mabel. Rather clever. Cheers.'

After the meal I made my apologies to Madge and Mabel and retreated to a quiet, secluded little beach bar Madge had recommended. I took a pen and notebook. I needed quiet and they understood. The beginnings of a synopsis was forming, and now was the time to get it down before the chit-chat, the sun, too many ideas and alcohol interfered.

The place was called 'Spyros' on the Sand' and that's exactly where I found myself, right on the beach, just far enough from the bar to have quiet and enough light, with a beer in hand and the sand beneath my feet watching the sun go down on the

Ionian Sea. I started scribbling down the concept: murder, of course, miscarriage of justice (that always works) dodgy local police, an eccentric in a mansion with a big cat...and two very nice, but quirky ladies who knew more about how Jimmy Finn operates than the man himself. I called it 'draft.' The title could come later. I'd think of something. Murder in the Dining Room? Murder on the menu? The Minestrone Murder? Whatever. I'd get the concept down tonight, peacefully, coherently. Then I'd contact the agent.

In the morning I was in luck. After breakfast young Philo alerted me to the hotel phone. It was him, the agent with a barrage: 'Have you got a synopsis now?' 'What's Jimmy Finn doing now?' 'Would Jimmy Finn really be sunning his backside away while there was a poison killer on the loose?' 'So, you're using this death in the hotel as an idea?' 'I like it. Hey, these calls aren't cheap. Just get me something I can send the critics so they'll get off my back.'

I spilled the idea to him. He was in a hurry, peak phone time in the UK. His feedback was mixed. 'Nice idea, nice villain, whichever one it is, any would do. But two elderly ladies? In Greece?'

'I'm in Greece. Your idea. Inspiration local.'

'That's not what our readers want. They want quiet English villages, English gentry, stabbings and bludgeons in the library or study, vicars, land owners, poachers as bad guys, quaint pub landlords and skulking figures outside the village as ruses to confuse the reader into diverting attention from the real killer who is actually someone of high profile in the village.'

'Predictable,' I said. 'The oldest and most predictable writing trick in the book. Everybody knows that the obvious bad guy at the beginning is not the bad guy. Sometimes it's the bad guy's friend – who's also a bad guy, which you didn't expect – but it's nearly always the guy who's squeaky clean. They want Cluedo. You sent me here. Your suggestion, your idea. I write on impulse. Location dictates. Maybe I don't like my readers. Maybe they need something new. Maybe they need two elderly ladies with a different outlook on life to shake things up.'

'Really, Angelo? Are you pissing me? You think the readers will go for that? For god's sake Fox, give me a break.'

I didn't tell him it was true, that Madge and Mabel existed. That would never work with him. I told him about a three-wheeled, two-stroke flatbed wagon with a shifty looking little man in red and black check socks under sandals. He slammed the phone down and left me in peace.

Me and the free wine.

Life's a beach.

12.

Whatever happened for the rest of the holiday, it seemed that Madge and Mabel were going to be inescapably part of it. Not that I minded. They had given me some inspiration for future writing, and despite what the agent said my heart was losing the will to present the same safe formula fiction I'd been churning like an assembly line production. I wanted something different to present and the other idea was having two elderly lady sleuths. I didn't think it had been done before. I could make it work.

In the meantime they both understood my need for space and isolation during the days. These I filled by walking the shores alone, listening to what English was picked up in bars, noting down interesting bits that could be used as dialogue in fiction and letting my mind run free, allowing some sort of storyline to form itself devoid of contrivance. The forced fiction of previous books the public learned to love I'd learned to hate, including my own books, and I was determined to give them something different. The mystery of what was happening in Gouvia was gold dust, if only I could extract it from a real life murder, multiple suspicious events and an explosion all in one small village. If I couldn't do that there was no hope. I wanted to find out more, unable to think what else I could do to find it and then consider that the truth – if it ever came out – might actually be more interesting than anything I could make up.

Thanos was on my mind a lot. So much that it interfered with my creative process. Thanos was real, larger than life, even. His reality was as big as anything I could create. He was a character I simply couldn't improve on. The urge to know more about him took over, impeding my writing flow.

That following evening Madge had a simple solution for my writer's block. 'Go back and see him.'

'And do what?' I said.

'Tell him the truth. That you're writing a novel and had been inspired by his character and could you please include him in it?'

'In my experience that's the quickest way to get someone to clam up,' I said. 'Sure, everyone wants to be in a novel. The problem is they start telling you what character they think they are and how to write them into it and befuddling the whole creative process. Characters are created covertly. You can base their characteristics on real people you've met, but you never tell them that, especially if you make them antagonists and you want the readers to hate them. They're just a springboard for development.'

'Then go back on some other pretence, like you did in the first place,' said Madge.

'He'll just talk property. That's not what I want. I want to talk about him and if I say I want to talk about him he'll get suspicious. And despite the hospitality and friendly demeanour, personally, I think he's got something to hide. And no one trusts a writer that asks too many questions. They seem to know exactly what you're up to. Trust me, I've tried it.'

We all went quiet for a while after that. Just the hum-drum of the few guests, the evening breeze and the soothing music floated through the dining room. It was a warmer evening than usual and the usual was hot. We sat near the open windows, flowing curtains waved to the breeze crossing our table and getting in some kind of fight with the overhead fan that seemed to be losing the will to turn. I was sat with my back to a window in a loose, white short-sleeved shirt and cotton khaki shorts wishing I hadn't bothered with underpants or my hat resting on the chair back. I wore sandals, no socks and plenty of Deet. Madge and Mabel looked enviably more comfortable in sleeveless floral summer dresses.

'Oh, let's just go out on the town tonight, shall we?' said Mabel. 'I could do with walking off the meal and find a nice bar with a working fan.'

So we went for a walk and looked for a nice bar. It was Niko's and it wasn't nice and the fan didn't work. Not on that night. The recently erected stage across the road in the field was in full swing. No music, just speeches in Greek, political banners, balloons and an angry audience blowing kazoos at any speaker or speech they didn't like. So we stayed and had a beer. This was about as exciting as it got in Gouvia and looked like a lot of fun. We sat and drank and Mabel did some translation. It was some kind of socialist party rally shouting about political corruption in government seeping its way down from central Greece and contaminating the very fabric of Corfu life. Sounded familiar. I was more interested in the animated looks on faces that reddened up with passion and booze. There looked to be more booze across the road than at Niko's. Niko himself wasn't amused at the loss of custom because of the noise. There were only two other people in the bar and they were getting up to leave. Across the road men were cracking them open, downing them and smashing them angrily into bins whenever they disagreed with a speaker. Even the angry dissenters of Corfu had more community pride than many back home. It was entertaining in a warped sort of way.

We'd had enough. It was impossible to have a conversation and we were going to leave after the first drink. That's when I saw him. He had his back partly to us at first, seated at the rear of the rally on the outside of the last row of bleachers. It's when he got up to leave and lifted his hat I recognised the hair. I recognised the height. The hair and beard just wasn't the Greek thing. He looked around briefly, looked around in a way that said he didn't want to be noticed looking around. He wiped his hair with a hanky and placed the straw Panama back on. He wore sunglasses, but I knew that build, that hair and the motions of a man acting furtively. He set off walking down the road in the direction away from our hotel. Walking with a gait like someone had kicked him hard. Too many coincidences. Another man joined him. I didn't get a proper look at that one.

And that's when hell came to Gouvia. I thought one of the amps across the road had blown at first. But no, no blown fuse sends pieces of wood, glass and fragments of banner flying. No blown fuse flattens out people with a fire-flash and plume of smoke. And no blown amp feels like someone had cup-slapped your ears. It was silent and eerie at first, like no one believed what had just happened. Those that weren't laid out on the grass suddenly started running about screaming. Bloodied faces appeared through smoke and cried out. Without any translation I quickly learned the Greek word for help. I got up to move and wanted to do something to help, but I figured any phone call for emergency assistance would be wasted in misunderstood translations and I could see Niko was already on to it.

I wanted to follow the man in the Panama hat and his friend and took off quickly in their direction. He was still in sight and walking casually as though nothing unusual had happened. An innocent man would at least turn around and look. And a guilty man would at least turn around and feign shock.

I was interrupted by a fat man with a cigar barring my way. He pushed his fat mitt to my chest halting my stride.

'Well, well, Mr. Plumpton?' said Castellanos. 'Where are you going?'

I pointed across his shoulder. 'I want to know where that man is going. And that's not my name as you well know.'

'Derek Plumpton. Mr. Derek Plumpton. Why don't you go

back to your two friends and mind your own business? There is nothing you can do here.'

'And nobody indulges in mockery in a disaster. My name is Fox and if you don't mind I'll be going thanks.'

I tried to go around him, but he just side-stepped me each time I tried.

'Leave now, Mr. Fox.' Castellanos' tone was less mockery, more threat this time. 'Everything is in hand here, now leave this to those who know how to deal with such situations.'

'Yeah...funny how you just happened to be here at the right time.'

'I take an interest in politics, Mr. Fox. Does that not surprise you? Every man in Greece is political one way or another. One could say it is very lucky I do so, wouldn't you say?'

I didn't say. Castellanos pulled at his fat turd of a cigar and tried to blow it in my direction. The breeze was in my favour. It blew back across his sweaty face, joining the other smoke drifting from the debris.

The man I wanted to follow had disappeared into the night. I heard sirens in the distance and returned to Madge and Mabel. They were helping the injured across the road to the bar. Niko was pushing tables together, laying out the injured and tearing up tablecloths as makeshift bandages. There was a lot of blood. Blood mixed with spilt beer and wine on tables and on the floor, sticky and slippery on the tiles. Niko was shouting instructions at anyone trying to help. A young man shuffled across the road, his hand pressed to his neck. I helped him onto a table. Blood seeped from the hand. He swayed and rolled back, passing out. The hand dropped away, overhanging the table and blood spurted from a hole in his neck, splattering my shorts. I grabbed the edge of the tablecloth trying to stem the flow from his neck. Ambulances and fire engines screamed their arrival. I don't know how many, I was out of it, out of my own body, stuck to the neck of a guy who'd probably let go of his soul already. A medic grabbed my arm and gently pushed me away, taking over.

And I wondered. I wondered what sort of human being walks away from such devastation as though nothing unusual had happened.

What sort of demon is that?

13.

'You'll need two of these,' said Mabel. 'I need two of these.'

Mabel's hands shook as she tipped the capsules from a plastic prescription bottle into her hand. A couple of them missed, slipping her fingers and spinning on the table. I picked one up, staring doubtfully at them in their blue and yellow gelatine casing.

'What are these?' I said.

'For insomnia,' said Mabel.

'It's a sad day when it comes to this,' said Madge. 'It's been a long time since Mabel had to resort to her medication.'

'A long time,' said Mabel. 'I'm so upset.'

We were back at the Aeres, sat in the empty dining room. It seemed like the whole of Gouvia had turned out to the scene of devastation not far away. There was so much going on we came away as emergency services were resorting to pushing back the good-intentioned people getting in the way. There was so much chaos and people were getting underfoot of the professionals. I had that feeling like I was as useful as an ashtray on a motorbike. I looked at my bloodied shorts and shirt and tried to convince myself that at least I tried.

I picked up the medicine bottle and read it. Sodium amytal, 500 mg. The rest of the info was illegible, the print was faded like the bottle had been carried around a while but hadn't been used. I guessed this was that rare occasion when it was about to be. 'Are these safe after alcohol?'

Mabel answered by throwing a couple to the back of her mouth and downing a gulp of wine.

'I think I'll pass,' I said. I handed the capsules back and Mabel shakily returned them to the bottle. 'I could do with a stiff brandy or three though.'

Christos and Philo came into the dining room and seemed

to have read my mind. Straight behind the bar Christos went and came out with a bottle of Metaxa and glasses. He came and sat with us and poured.

Christos had a bandaged hand. 'Burnt,' he said. 'I burnt my hand on a man's trousers. He was still smoking like a log on a fire. I heard the bang and went to look and tried to help, but the fireman made me go away.'

'It's probably right of them to do so,' said Madge. 'With the best of intentions some of us were getting in the way. It's what they'd do back home I suppose. Heroes and fools are often indistinguishable in times of crisis.'

'But these are my people,' said Christos. 'I feel so helpless. I don't know what is happening in Gouvia. Why is God doing this to us? What have we done?' He poured me another brandy. The first had gone down already. He had eyes like a beaten dog cowering before its master.

'Maybe God has had no part in this,' I said. 'Maybe someone just didn't like the politics on show tonight.'

'What are you saying, Mr. Fox? In Gouvia people have different politics. They get angry, as does everyone everywhere when they don't agree. In Gouvia they argue over drinks, go to bed and shake hands in the morning over coffee and toast. This is Gouvia, a peaceful place. There are no mafias in Gouvia. What are you saying?'

'I'm not saying anything. Sure...nice people in Gouvia. I guess one of the amplifiers blew up then. It probably caught one of those bottles used to fill the balloons.' I was good at lying to myself but didn't feel good about it. 'Where's Elena tonight?' I asked. I didn't want Christos or anyone else taking anything from my suggestion there was any human motive for the explosion. Not yet.

'Elena is in sorrow,' said Christos. 'She's gone to her bedroom to weep for us and pray. She said to me tonight we should have sold the Aeres before.'

87

'Before when? Why would you want to sell this beautiful place?'

'Because the Aeres will finish. Gouvia is finished now. First guests have left because of Mr. Barton, now this.'

I could say the room fell silent, but it didn't, only the people inside. When the conversation stopped, the sounds from Gouvia and Niko's Tavern, cries of sirens and victims and saviours drifted in by the flowing curtains. I wanted to shut it out, but sweat rolled off me.

Mabel finished her brandy and left for bed, mumbling that her medication might take effect soon.

'What did you mean?' I asked Christos. 'Why should you have sold the Aeres before? You couldn't have known these things were to happen.'

'Men came here once,' said Christos. 'Nice men, they were. They were well dressed, in suits, very gentle and well spoken. They knew a lot about Gouvia and were very admiring of our hotel. They said they were agents for buyers from the Greek mainland, from Athens they said. They said development of Gouvia was most necessary for the progress of the island and the financial "infrastructure," they called it. I asked what this word means. They said it means the wealth and future of Gouvia would be secured forever. There would be no more poverty on the island, no people without homes like you see in Corfu town sometimes, and security and jobs for all. And wouldn't that be a good thing for Gouvia? They said. And how could we refuse to help our fellow citizens of our fair island? They said. And then they made us an offer on the hotel – a very good offer. More than the Aeres was worth. An offer they said only a fool could possibly refuse.'

'Who were they?' I asked.

'I don't know for certain,' said Christos. 'There are rumours, but the people here are frightened of saying names and the police don't want to help. But Mama had worked so hard to keep the Aeres going after Father had passed. It was what he would have wanted, she says. She looked at all of us, to see our faces and she knew then that we wanted to stay here forever. When we refused the men's mood changed, they called us fools and selfish to reject the opportunity to let the island grow and develop and to help the poor. In the end it was Tobias that sent them on their way. He escorted them to the door, when one of them turned and spat at Tobias' feet. Tobias slapped the man hard across the face at this insult. The man said Tobias and the Aeres was cursed.'

'How long ago was this?' I asked.

'A year, maybe. Others in Gouvia have been asked to sell. Some have done so; the offers have been good. But not Mama. This is our home. This was our father's dream, not just a home, but his dream he worked so hard for. How could Mama sell a man's dream as though it could have a price? Love does not have a price, wouldn't you agree, Mr. Fox?'

I agreed and went to bed. A strange bed in a foreign land. A bed of lucid dreams of death, blood and cigar smoke. I slept little.

In the morning church bells drifted in my bedroom window, ringing out slow and mournfully, a beat so slow you thought it must have stopped after each strike, but then it would strike again with an echo and a dreadful long silence after. A silence between so complete nothing else stirred, no street-life, no vehicles sounded.

I despised life – all life – my own included. I hated my own sense of inadequacy and helplessness. I went to the dining room early and had coffee. I couldn't eat. When you feel this lousy about life there's only one of two things you can do. Do something about it, or end it all.

I finished my coffee and asked for a handful of Mabel's sodium amytal capsules and a length of rope.

14.

I owed my agent a phone call, so I gave him one on his expense. He wasn't happy about it. He was less happy at my reason for the call.

'How much does a fully grown adult male cheetah weigh?' I asked.

A long silence followed. *'Are you pissing me about again, Fox? If you're serious go to a library.'*

'The books here are written in Greek. The people reading them here are Greek. That's why they're written in Greek. Find out for me and ring back.'

'So, you're writing about two elderly ladies, a two-stroke whatever truck driver and a cheetah? Great. Sounds like a Booker Prize winner, I'm sure.' He snorted the last sentence.

'It's in the story. Trust me, just find out and get back.'

'This better be good.' He hung up.

The next part was tricky.

'Why do you want so many?' Mabel asked.

'I can't sleep,' I said. 'I just need a few to tide me over for the next few nights. Did you sleep alright last night?'

'Well, yes. They are quite effective at calming one down. And I do feel more relaxed this morning, but oh, that dreadful thing last night. How can one forget? No pills can wipe that out. I don't think I'll ever get over it.'

Mabel sipped her morning coffee. She had a look of doubt written all over her face. She put her cup down and reached into her bag for the plastic bottle. She shook two capsules out onto a napkin. 'I'll give you two. Then you can see if they're the right thing for you. Heaven forbid that I should knock you out and numb your writing brain.' Madge had the same doubtful face.

'I think that will be fine,' I said. 'Two to be taken at bedtime, is that right? Would that put me to sleep for the night?'

'Oh, yes,' said Mabel. 'Two, then give it a few minutes, put your head down and you're lights out.'

'Thank you. I'll try them tonight.'

I didn't try them. I asked for two more the following day. And two more the day after that.

'Up to one-hundred and fifty pounds.' The agent replied the day after I rang him.

'About the weight of the average lean man, then?' I said.

'You're writing a book on African wildlife now?'

'No, I'm writing a thriller about a big cat that terrorizes a Greek island. The local police chief is at odds with the Mayor who wants to open the beaches on the 4th of July. I'm calling it "Claws."'

'Don't be funny, Fox. Just keep Jimmy Finn alive for me, thanks.' He hung up before it cost him too much. He forgets that Jimmy Finn pays his wages.

I asked Christos for a length of rope. He asked if I wanted the Land Rover as well. I said no, just a length or rope. 'You do have some rope?' I asked. 'You rescued a motorbike from an olive tree in the mountains earlier in this season. A couple of those Club 18-30 rascals launched themselves off the hillside. You and Philo dragged it back up the hill with your Land Rover, if I'm not mistaken.'

'Yes, that is correct,' said Christos. 'But please...you are going to do what with it?'

'I can't say, at least not yet.'

'For anyone else, Mr. Fox, I would say no. But you I trust. You are this writer person, I have heard and very respected in your country. For this I trust you. You may tell me later.'

'Sounds like the two ladies have spilled the beans on me then.'

'They tell me about you, yes. The two ladies, they are so fond of you, but I don't say anything to anyone else in the Aeres. They know you want to be private and not pestered by other guests and I respect your privacy, Mr. Fox.'

Christos led me out to the hotel garage. From the back of the Rover he pulled out a bundle of heavy duty ropes. I selected one I thought to be about thirty feet in length.

I asked for a hook. A big one. He showed me a coupling link – like a hook, but not a hook – a thing used to link a rope with after wrapping it around the front wheel of a motorbike. It wasn't what I wanted. I tried to explain how I was going to approach my adventure without giving it away and he said to give him an hour. An hour later he came back with a hook. Two hooks, in the form of a two-pronged dinghy anchor. Ideal.

'Just one more thing, if you can oblige me,' I said. 'I need a piece of meat. A piece of raw meat. A large piece of raw meat. Fresh meat. And a knife.'

15.

I was lying on my back on a lounger by the pool, looking through my fingers trying to imagine shapes in the only two clouds I'd ever seen in the sky above Gouvia. They hung there, two round cotton wool blobs with no other shape than round or oval, not going anywhere fast. If the Greeks came up with the notion of Gods and deities by looking at the sky they didn't get it in the daytime in Gouvia. If there had never been night their gods would have been fluffy sheep gods with no face or feet.

A shadow blocked the sheep. 'What are you really up to, Mr. Fox?' said Christos. 'Are you fishing? For a big fish?'

'You could say that,' I said.

'Why do you need meat? This I don't understand. Is this a bribe for someone? Is this about Tobias?'

I sat upright at that. 'You're pretty clever and you're working on me, that's for certain. You really think I'm going to get Tobias out of jail with a hook and a lump of meat? I don't know how that would work.'

'You must tell me, please. I want to help.'

I had to confess. 'I'm going to try and get into the Thanos' mansion. The Liontari Ilion. To dig up some dirt on Hector Thanos. Maybe there's something about Tobias. That would be good, but I wouldn't count on it. That's not what I'm doing it for. It's all a hunch, a suspicion I have about things. I hope you understand.'

Christos smiled at me. It started as a frown, like I'd said something really stupid. His brow furled and his mouth widened into a broad crescent. The kind of smile you get that's neither approving nor disapproving. The kind of smile you get when you tell a joke that has a fart in it somewhere.

'You are a fool,' said Christos. 'But I will help. But no one must know I helped.'

I explained the rest, I owed Christos that much for being obliging. I told him about my first meeting with Thanos and my suspicions – strong, but so far unfounded and my suspicions of Castellanos.

'Bent copper,' said Christos. 'Everybody here thinks so. Castellanos comes here sometimes and expects free drinks and meals in our Taverns, even our own. The people here comply because he has too much power. He can revoke our business licenses or not approve them for renewal when the time comes. All he has to do is say something like this business or that business is cheating the clients or faking the finances and reports this to the magistrates who deny the application. I think he even takes money from some here.'

'I didn't know that,' I said. 'But it doesn't surprise me.'

'I think he, how you say in your country...he stitch Tobias up. Tobias could not have done what Castellanos says.'

'Well, that's another matter. It's very possible Castellanos could have and I'd love to prove that.'

'Then you will let me help?'

'I don't think so, Christos. It's unlikely I'll find anything related to Tobias anyway. I just have this instinctive feeling that Thanos knows something about the recent events here.' I was tempted to mention that I thought I saw him leaving the political rally after the explosion, but that would have got Christos' blood up, I'm sure. I would have to explain Charlie as well. It was obvious he didn't know about Charlie, otherwise he would have guessed the meat part. No, it wasn't a good idea.

'Jimmy Finn always works alone,' I told him. 'He's very discreet and silent as a mouse when he wants to be. It's what I've learned as a writer...but never put it into practice...until now. I hope you understand. Besides, I doubt Elena would approve.'

'Mama doesn't have to know. This is a man's task.'

'Elena would certainly know if we got caught. She would be heartbroken to see another member of her family arrested. I, on the other hand would rely on public outcry from back home if I was arrested, or even some sort of 'celebrity immunity.' I'm certain my agent would work something out for me.'

Who was I kidding?

'I understand,' Christos said. 'If you change your mind, I'm here.'

'You must say nothing to the two ladies,' I said. 'They are my friends and will only try to talk me out of it.'

Christos smiled and made a zipped up mouth gesture before shaking my hand. 'Good luck, Mr. Fox...I mean Mr. Jimmy Finn.'

16.

I was sat in my room at the wobbly as a crème caramel table staring at a lump of raw prime beef the size of my head. Christos had delivered it to my room after everyone had retired for the night. I'd asked for pork, but couldn't explain to Christos why and they hadn't got any in the kitchen anyway. I got a penknife out of my pocket to stab the joint then put it away. Later, I thought.

I was out at 1:15 AM. Gouvia was mostly silent, the last of the bars were a mere hum of chatter from the late night drinkers and the dancing table Greek Zorbas had gone to bed. Even the Club 18-30 dive down the road was silent, which was strange. I figured they'd gone out to some beach somewhere playing chase the beer can into the sea at night without drowning. I pushed the bike out about half a mile from town where it was so silent you could hear every moth trying to bash its brains out on a lone street lamp before starting it up. I rechecked everything one last time: Rope, pills, joint of beef, Kodak Ektra with new film. Then I was away on my rehired, pulls to the left, dragged out of an olive tree motorbike, on a warm breeze leaving behind a trail of night-flyers trying to follow the joint.

I took another route plotted from a map this time, westward of Liontari Ilion and approached it from the North, thus avoiding driving past the gate and risk awakening Thanos. I came to a halt, killing the engine and pushed the motorbike into some woods. I guessed I was about a mile away from the mansion, from where the engine's sound would be heard no louder than a mosquito hum.

I took the sack out of the pannier – rope, anchor, meat and pills and proceeded with my plan. Lighting my pocket torch, I stabbed the beef joint four times – two on each side. Into each hole I inserted one of Mabel's sodium amytal capsules.

'Sorry, Charlie,' I whispered. 'But I just can't risk it.'

I'd thought very carefully about it. Two for a beast the weight of an average man to sleep. Four would surely knock him out. And a fit, lithe creature like Charlie would surely come to no harm from a slight overdose. I considered using all six capsules, but I didn't know enough about them, only what Mabel had told me. So I stuck another one in.

Then I walked it by the road with a sack over my shoulder on a moonless, but clear night, a night like I'd never seen, a night on a road lit by the bright streak of the Milky Way across the sky accompanied by the melodious chirping of cicadas. Around a bend the light of Thanos' drive came into view, the road illuminated by the English-style carriage lampposts, highlighting the night-flyers ahead. I turned into some olive trees, somewhere near where I'd parked the bike the first time and felt my way to the side wall, my only guide being the feeble starlight that threw faint patches here and there across the grassy woodland floor. I followed the wall down, getting deeper into the trees until I guessed I was somewhere opposite Thanos' citrus orchard. I was in luck. The ground level rose up there, the remnants of early ground works, I assumed, shortening the height of the wall.

Again, I had to light the torch, holding it in my mouth and realising the one big stupid mistake I'd made in all the preplanning. The rope was too thick to tie around the joint. I could get it around, alright, and tie a knot, but it wouldn't tie tight enough to squeeze into the meat far enough to hold the joint fast and secure. I tried it and tested it, but each time I lifted it, the meat would slip out. It just wouldn't hold. I needed string. Why hadn't I considered string, string to wrap tightly around the joint first and then to the rope? Jimmy Finn would never do anything so dumb. I could hear Mabel's voice scolding me.

Shoelace. The only option apart from abandoning the night. I slipped it out from my left shoe. Just long enough to wrap around once with enough spare to attach to the rope. I wrapped it as hard as I could, the lace digging deep into the soft, spongy meat. I made a noose with the rope and tied the joint to it with the lace. I looped the other end of the rope into the anchor's eye, finishing with a bowline knot.

Three attempted shots later, the anchor snagged the wall ledge on the far side. I tested it three times, tugged it, yanked it and pulled myself up part way, satisfied it wasn't going anywhere without whipping it out from its lodging.

Then Jimmy Finn did what he does best, but Derek Plumpton hadn't done since high school P.E. classes and got a D minus in. But I managed it. Feet against the wall, I walked it up, Batman style until the rope to wall distance got too short. Then I dangled. I wrapped my left foot around the rope so it draped over the top of it, then pressed my right foot onto the rope (I remembered something useful from PE) and pulled myself up, grasped the ledge with my left hand and got my right elbow over. I grabbed the anchor with my left hand and scrambled my right leg over the top. I was there, face down and staring at the shadow of a thick tree bough overhanging the wall a few metres away and hearing Mabel's voice again. I wasn't Jimmy Finn, just an old man panting and wheezing like a forge bellows and breaking the night song of the cicadas.

I gave myself a minute before sitting up. I hoisted the beef joint up, re-fixed the anchor to the outside edge of the wall and lowered the beef down to somewhere near ground level. I let it dangle, like a fisherman dangling a lure just above the water. Then I waited like a fisherman.

I was fine, I was sure. This wasn't some cat burglary in London's Knightsbridge. This was one man alone in a house the size of a music hall, unlikely to see or hear anything and would be asleep. I hoped to God.

It didn't take long. The sleek silhouette of Charlie emerged from the trees below. I heard him sniffing. I pulled the rope up a little, but Charlie soon located it. He didn't go for it straight away. I think he was curious, but being cautious. This was something new to him, I could tell. He wasn't stupid. He put his paws up against the wall, but didn't jump. He just watched. I think he was purring. I'd heard him sniffing. I knew what he wanted and how. I remembered what Thanos had said about cheetahs not being scavengers.

The meat was within reach of a good jump, but Charlie didn't identify with it as prey. Thanos probably never offered him a cow. So I did what all good anglers do, like a fly-fisherman flicking a line with a lure across the river surface, I swung the bait back and forth. I raised it a little higher, higher than I thought Charlie could jump. Charlie crouched and backed away. Then he did a wide circular turn and disappeared into the trees and I thought he'd lost interest. A few seconds elapsed and a black bolt shot from the trees and leapt at the bait, taking me by surprise. Charlie had both his paws and mouth clamped onto the joint so securely and suddenly, he nearly pulled me off the wall. But my plan worked. The shoelace knot gave and both predator and prey fell in a tumble to the ground. Charlie shook his prize like it was a live thing. He shook it and threw it and chased it. Then he laid front down holding it with his paws, panting, before disappearing with it into the citrus trees.

I waited. I had one of those wonderful modern inventions called a luminous dial watch on my wrist emitting its eerie green and quite safe radioactive glow. I timed half an hour, about the time Mabel had said her capsules took to work. I waited longer, I had to be certain. An hour passed. Now I had to get to work.

I checked the anchor, tugging it hard, digging into the stone wall. I grabbed it by the shank with my right hand and the rope with the other hand I let go of the anchor and slipped bit by bit to the ground.

The rear of Thanos' mansion had a ghostly pallor to it in the starlight against the dark of the windows like the eyeholes of a skull. I made my way to the bay sashes. I figured that Thanos didn't bother locking them with a guard like Charlie in the yard. I was right, and in luck. From the lawn I couldn't see the lock of the one I tried. I was chest high to the sill, but the first prise of my pen knife told me it was free and ready to slide up. I prised it just enough to get both sets of fingers under and with a little bit of juggling it rode up and I climbed through.

Now was the part that really worried me. I switched on the torch to an almost empty room. Apart from the plants, everything I'd hoped to find was gone. The table where Charlie had followed me around was gone and more disappointingly, the bureau where Thanos had his property files, and where I'd hoped to find anything else he hadn't shown me. I should have guessed, if the window isn't locked, there's nothing to find. I heard Mabel in my head again. What would Jimmy Finn do? He'd look further. Thanos had shifted it for a reason and that reason seemed suspicious. Or maybe he kept any real dirt on himself hidden in unlikely places?

I made my way room by room, at least on the ground floor. I hadn't the nerve of Jimmy Finn to sneak upstairs, not knowing which of the bedrooms was occupied by Hector Thanos. Every room was bare. This was more than Minimalism (or was it less?) I expected at least some modern furniture, bookshelves or functional fittings. Was he moving out? And why?

I was intrigued now, so intrigued I swept through every corner of each room looking for that elusive secret hiding place, hidden hatch or cubby hole where every one of Jimmy

Finn's villains kept their secrets. But that was fiction and I was the villain right now, sneaking around someone's home in the middle of the night illegally and gaining in confidence while doing it.

And finding nothing.

Maybe the kitchen? One of Jimmy Finn's villains kept his dirty little secrets in a hidden compartment at the bottom of a chest freezer. I slipped silently around from the last room on the ground floor, through the main hall, past the staircase, through the reception room and downstairs to the kitchen and found a couple of dirty little secrets just as I was about to call it a night.

I wasn't expecting it. A small cupboard within a cupboard was hidden from view by an array of spice jars. I carefully cleared the obstructing jars to the worktop. It was locked, the typical skeleton key type of lock with a gunmetal face, but no key was visible. But I had a comb and a previous lesson in picking from a locksmith. You learn a lot researching how villains work. I took my comb out and with the meat stabbing knife, cut half of the nylon teeth out and inserted the prong end. I fiddled it back and forth, twisting it clockwise at various depths until I felt the lever lift. The deadbolt slid back and I pulled the door open. Jimmy Finn was in.

Several more jars and small bottles were inside. One jar contained crystals, a little like salt. I thought it odd. I'd already moved a large labelled container of salt aside. The other jars intrigued me. All were unlabelled. One had a liquid inside, like clear oil and small lumps of what appeared to be metal of some sort. I thought they were lead. But lead in oil? I unscrewed the top and sniffed. It was like mineral oil, the smell reminded me of an engineering works I once visited in my research for a story.

One bottle was unmistakable. I unscrewed the top and smelled it. It was one of two things, either almond essence or arsenic. Arsenic smells of almond, a bitter almond scent. Jimmy Finn knew that. I tried to relate this thought to Tobias, but Tobias had supposedly used strychnine on Dave Barton.

I decided to take photos, of the kitchen, the bottles; the whole secret little layout with hidden cupboard. I took lots of photos. I reckoned I'd rolled off most of a 24 frame cassette, a lot of snapping and flashing in the night that left me blinded and nervous. But unless Thanos was in the room with me, I convinced myself I was safe. Then I decided to take the suspicious bottle and jar. I only had two pockets and the one with the oil and metal or whatever else it was worried me somewhat, but still intrigued me. It was something that just didn't belong in a kitchen cupboard. Nor was arsenic, if that's what it was. I even wondered if the metallic substance could be something radioactive, but I doubted that. Even someone like Thanos wouldn't be able to get hold of that. But I had the feeling it was something important, something to do with Thanos' causing mayhem in Gouvia.

So I opened it. I fingered a piece of the metal out onto the worktop. I was tempted to wrap it up in a hanky and stuff it into my pocket, but something told me the oil it was in was important. I looked around in the little cupboard, then in the larger cupboards for a container small enough for a sample. And then I found them: phials. Lots of phials. Castellanos said he'd found a 'phial' of strychnine in Tobias' room. Lots of little screw-cap phials like every good cook doesn't use in a kitchen. I unscrewed one and put the metal sample in and poured enough of the oil in to cover it and screwed it back up, wrapped it in a hanky and stuffed it into the little side-slip pocket of my khakis. I took a spoonful of the crystals into another phial and a sample of the almond-smelling bottle, pouring it very carefully into another and put them both into my big pockets.

This was a job for the police, but not Castellanos. Nor

anyone he was associated with. For all I knew his entire force might be corrupt. My best bet would be to get in touch with the guys from mainland Greece even if I had to travel there. But could I trust even them? I would have to mention Castellanos by name and admit to how I got the phials and photos. They might be interested, but they were illegally gained. I could tell my agent, but he'd just demand I return home immediately. I had detective friends in the police back home. One in particular – a guy called Dreyfus – I'd befriended in my research into the character of Jimmy Finn. He'd laughed at my questions back then, but was very helpful and had access to pretty well every criminal file in the world. I was sure he wouldn't laugh at me this time. This was real, I was certain it was hard evidence of someone with criminal intentions. If I could I'd get a chemist while still on the island to analyse the phials before proceeding. I'd get the UK newspapers involved. The bottles were unlabelled, but had Thanos written all over them, with a scribbling of Castellanos. They might as well have said: 'to be used against suckers like Tobias Teresi' written on instructions.

It was time for me to go. I made my way out retracing my way by torchlight to the big room with the sash bay windows and slipped out. I tried to close it behind me. It was stuck. I wasn't about to force it. The thought that it might suddenly give and slam down in the middle of the night was too risky, so I had to leave it open. Thanos would know someone had been in, but I reckoned I'd unlikely be a suspect. More likely he'd think an opportunistic thief had been attracted by the wealth of the place and been disappointed on entry. And I doubted if he'd notice any difference with his kitchen cupboards. Unless he counted the phials.

I slipped silently across the lawns, delicately, elegantly as a ballerina to my rope, still clutching my trusty Kodak Ektra. I was terrified and proud of myself at the same time. I kissed the camera. 'Gotcha,' I whispered before stuffing it into my back pocket.

I had one foot on the wall and two hands on the rope when I heard a rustle, which made me slip onto my back. Two yellow-amber glowing eyes hovered over me and I froze. I heard purring, purring so loud it blocked the night call of the cicadas. Charlie lay down on his front and placed one paw on my chest. He licked his other paw then licked my face. He was thanking me for the feast.

'Not now, Charlie,' I whispered. The pills hadn't worked. I should have guessed. Charlie was a fit, robust predator with a heart of steel, and gold it seemed. He was thanking me in a way I didn't like but didn't protest. I stroked his head and shoulder and tried to move. 'Let me up now, Charlie.' I took his paw and slowly removed it. 'Good boy, Charlie.' I got up and grabbed the rope and Charlie nudged me on the thigh.

I bent down to give him one last stroke of his head. He looked up at me and his paw reached out to pat my foot. I said my goodbye. 'So long, Charlie,' I whispered. 'It was nice meeting you. Perhaps we'll meet again one day.'

Then the thing I most dreaded happened. A loud bang came from the mansion. As loud as a gunshot. That's the trouble with sash windows; you can't trust them when they stick. If that counterweight cord is frayed – and you just can't tell from the outside – they can drop at any time. Now my head-Mabel was telling me Jimmy Finn would have propped it open with a stick. Jimmy Finn doesn't usually carry sticks about his person.

Charlie spun around like a startled kitten and I panicked. I took the opportunity of his distraction and leapt onto the rope and scrambled myself up, losing my left, lace-less shoe in the process. I couldn't go back. I just had to get away. I threw myself onto the wall top and tried to pull the rope up. Charlie had hold of it in his jaw. He was chewing and playing with it like a cat on a string. Traces of the joint must have attracted him and every time he let go and I pulled, he'd leap up and get it like a cat. It was too far for me to jump. Maybe in the daylight I might have chanced it, but I couldn't see the ground and would have no idea when to brace myself.

A light came on in the mansion and I yanked the rope one last time as Charlie released it. I repositioned the anchor to the inside, tested it with a couple of yanks and slid, almost fell down the outside wall. I gave the rope a few whip-flicks to release the anchor, but it wasn't coming. And I wasn't staying. There was no time to lose and I left it.

I don't know how long I stumbled through the woods, but it seemed a lifetime. I got lost. I couldn't locate the motorbike, despite risking the torch to light my way. In the end I went too far and bypassed the place I'd left it. I had to sneak out to the road to get my bearings. The road was empty and silent. I realised I'd gone too far then and made my way back down towards the mansion by starlight, my ears pricked up like a bat, it felt.

I found it, wheeled it out to the road and I was gone, hardly believing my luck that I hadn't been seen.

The first delicate rays of daylight lightened the sky in pink on a warm but comfortable morning as I rode into Gouvia. By the time I arrived my left foot was sore from changing gear with only a sock on. I stopped at the outskirts of the village and wheeled the bike the rest of the way to the Aeres. The hotel was silent and dark inside the reception area as I slipped past the desk to the stairs up to the rooms.

I walked into a wall. Not a hard wall but a soft one. A wall of lard. An ugly cigar stinking wall of lard. A light came on and Deet stood in a corner, his hand over the switch.

Castellanos stood barring my way like a big moustached gorilla, only not as handsome. He held out his hand. 'Camera,' he said.

I handed over my trusty Ektra with all its evidence.

'Now turn around.'

I turned around and Castellanos rifled my pockets. Castellanos took the phials. Game over.

'It seems, Mr. Derek Plumpton, that you have lost one of your shoes. Well, here's one that you will find a good fit.

And with that he gave me one good hard kick in the rear I felt all the way to my fingertips. I got angry, but had to stifle it. As Deet and Castellanos dragged me arm in arm outside, beyond Deet's sniggering was the faint sound of Elena somewhere nearby, sobbing.

17.

I was shoved in the back of Castellanos' police vehicle. Deet handcuffed me. We didn't go to any police station, rather the Courthouse and holding cells where I'd last seen Tobias. The same surly-looking duty officer as last time sat filling out forms in Greek for me to sign whether I understood them or not. Castellanos shoved a pen in my free hand, I signed and then he shoved me still cuffed to Deet, towards the holding cells door.

'I'm allowed a phone call,' I said. 'No matter what crap you've made me sign, I know I'm allowed a phone call. And when my agent finds out you didn't allow me one, he'll be straight onto the Consulate.'

Castellanos sniffed like a dog that's stepped in its own shit and doesn't know what to do. He snapped his fingers at the duty officer who slid the desk phone over.

I picked up the receiver. 'UK,' I said. 'And it's private.'

Castellanos shook his head. 'No,' he said.

'Aeres Hotel then.' Deet uncuffed me and I dialled the number and Christos answered. He already knew. I was going to ask him to phone my agent, but Castellanos put his finger on the plunger and hung up for me before Christos could agree.

'It won't help you, Fox,' said Castellanos. 'You had to stick your nose into Corfu business, didn't you? I understand that you want a story, but you crossed a line. Why? You have nothing. What did you expect to find?'

'I found something, alright,' I said. 'And that's why you confiscated it. Maybe I know Thanos is a crook. Maybe he's to do with the explosion at the rally by Niko's, or any of the other weird events in Gouvia. Maybe you're covering for him. Maybe you're taking backhanders from him, just like you help yourself to free food and drinks to keep the hoteliers sweet.'

Castellanos drew his hand back and swiped me across the face. I felt a trickle from my nose that ran down to my lips. I licked them and tasted salt. I wiped my finger under my nose. It was blood, alright. I was still stinging from the boot to my ass. My instinct was to slap him right back in the face.

So I slapped him right back in the face.

The last time I got dived on was in a dog-pile at high school when our team scored a late winning goal in the school's county cup. They didn't include punches then. Castellanos, Deet and the duty officer all wrestled me to the floor. Castellanos straddled me; his fat arse took the wind out of my lungs. He slapped me back and forth. I knew he didn't want to punch me proper; bent cops don't work that way, in Greece or anywhere else. No bruises – no comeback, diplomatic or not. He wanted to hurt me with no evidence of it. So he slapped me like a woman slaps an errant husband and kept slapping. I tried to cover my face, but Deet and the duty officer held my arms out while Castellanos did his scorned wife impression. I reckon a minute of this passed at least, with regular breaks to catch his fat man's breath.

Castellanos stood up and brushed himself off. Deet yanked me up. Castellanos was still catching his breath when he jabbed a finger into my chest. 'Don't fuck with me Mr. Derek Plumpton. You are in so much trouble now. No one fucks with Elias Castellanos, I have power and authority here. Do not forget that. Now take him away.'

Deet and the duty officer grabbed me by the arms and shoved me down the cell hall to the sixth door on the left and pushed me inside. An exact duplicate of Tobias' cell, a pull-down wall bed, chair, toilet, sink and Greek graffiti that must have been funny to other Greeks who had scribbled laughing stick men pointing at balloon scripts. A few minutes later the serving hatch on the door opened and a tray holding a flannel, towel, some gauze and a bar of soap was pushed through. I bathed my face in the sink with the one cold tap, pulled down the bed and lay down holding the gauze under my nose which had started trickling again. I fell asleep. The pain from Castellanos' beating still stung, but I'd already been awake for a whole night.

I awoke late afternoon. The duty officer was serving out a meagre meal of bread, ham, cheese, some fruit and coffee which was shoved through the hatch. I ate, drank coffee and blew a large blood clot from my nose into some toilet roll. I lay back down, deflated. It was over and I was beaten and felt foolish, and if Castellanos hadn't kicked me already I would have done it myself. I slept again, my last thought was a hope that word had got back home and the bollocking I was going to get from my agent and eventual release. I had the beginnings of a story, but that's all it would ever be. I'd got what he wanted, but not what I wanted, some truth and justice.

Evening had come when I awoke again. I scolded myself for sleeping so long, thinking I'd be awake all night now. I could hear other inmates talking to each other, some laughing, another sounded to be sobbing.

I called out: 'Tobias...Tobias...is that you?'

A voice answered: 'Hey mister, you are English?'

'Yes,' I replied. 'Are you Tobias? Tobias Teresi?'

'No, mister, my name is Nikoli. Who are you? What is an English man doing in Corfu jail?'

Another voice answered: 'He is English. English boys drink too much and get into trouble all the time here.'

'No, I didn't,' I replied to this other inmate. 'I didn't drink anything. I was in the wrong place at the wrong time.'

'Maybe you were found in the ladies room, eh?'

There was laughter from the other cells.

'No, of course not,' I said. 'I would do no such thing. But what about Tobias? Is he here? Tobias, are you in here, it's me,

Angelo. Answer me if you can.'

Tobias didn't answer, but Nikoli did: 'Tobias is gone, sir. He's not here anymore. He's gone up the hill to the big prison.'

My heart sank. 'What happened?' But I knew already. I imagined how bit by bit, Castellanos would have worn him down with threats and promises until Tobias' will was broken and he confessed with the hope of a court's sympathy, just like Castellanos had implied the last time I'd visited the jail. Everything I'd seen in the past twenty-four hours, from the contents of Thanos' kitchen to Castellanos' brutality, had reversed my view of Tobias. I wished now that I'd never said to Elena that I thought he must have done it, and now I couldn't wait to get out and tell her and the boys what I'd found...with no proof of it left.

'They take him away two days ago,' said Nikoli. 'He was found guilty and now he's in the big house. He is waiting for sentence. It doesn't sound good for him. If you murder a man here on Corfu, you will never get out. Did you know Tobias, sir?'

'Yes...yes, I did know him,' I whispered. 'I did know him.' I said it louder. 'He was innocent. He was damned well innocent!' I shouted it. 'Damned well innocent and one way or another I'll find out how he was stitched up!'

'Skasse!' The cry came from the end of the hall. I needed no translation. So we all shut up. Then the lights went out, but the talking carried on in whispers that floated the hall between cells. The last words I caught were in English. 'Castellanos...he bent,' the voice said. I hadn't even mentioned his name. They knew.

The following morning my cell door opened and my missing shoe was thrown in. A new duty officer was on the morning shift. 'Compliments of Hector Thanos,' he said. An hour later a tray with a couple of croissants and coffee appeared through the hatch. I heard grumbles float the hall. Discontent is a universal language. They were complaining about the meagre servings. I ate mine ravenously and was still hungry. What I wouldn't have given for a piece of cake-thick omelette and a plate of blancmange.

I tried jumping up to the little barred window, but there was nothing to see, the paved courtyard, a few road signs and roadside brush and a lot of hazy morning sunshine. I despaired. There was nothing for it but wait it out until my hearing. I had no idea how long that would be and the morning duty officer had no idea.

'It depends,' he said. 'We have a backlog of cases here. It can take days or weeks. Who knows?'

'I bet Castellanos knows,' I said. 'It seems to me that Tobias was rushed out of here and up the hill in no time at all. Why?'

'I don't know, sir. Maybe you should say nothing more now. It won't be good at your hearing if you continue to show disrespect to the authorities here.'

He was right. There was nothing for it but to lay here and rot. So I lay there imagining myself as a fallen tree in a forest, not dead but dying and waiting for the rot to set in. It was already happening. I didn't even want to talk to the others. My only hope was my agent. Legally he couldn't do anything, only appeal and plead with the British Consulate here for sympathy. Good luck with that.

That afternoon I was awoken from my rotten slumber by a turn of key and a creak of metal as my cell door swung open. The duty officer stood in the doorway. 'Get up, Mr. Fox. You are free to go.'

I sat up. Then I lay back down. Maybe this was one of Castellanos' cruel tricks. Maybe he'd instructed the duty officer into his cruelty. Castellanos was capable of it. I'd get up and the officer would slam the door in my face.

'What is wrong, Mr. Fox?' said the officer. 'Did you not hear me?'

'I heard you alright. What's the catch?'

'No catch. Someone is here to take you home. Maybe you should get up before they change their mind.'

I got up and cautiously approached him. He stood aside to let me through and followed me up the cell hall. I was confused and still half asleep, thinking it strange that my agent or a Consulate representative would get here so quick. My agent wouldn't have rushed and it would be pushing it to catch a plane here that soon and the Greeks – even British Consulate ones – don't do anything in a hurry.

What I got was the last person I expected. Sat by the duty officer's desk was Madge in a knee length blue, white lily patterned shift dress and white Raffia hat wafting her face with an oriental paper fan.

'My god, Angelo,' she said standing. 'You look awful. What the hell have you been up to?'

'It's a long story.'

'Well do tell. I've heard some of it, but I don't believe it.'

'Thank you,' I stuttered. I was still confused. 'How did you swing it? How much was my bail?'

'Bail?' said Madge. 'Good heavens, Angelo. You really aren't yourself, are you? How can you get bail when you haven't yet even had a hearing?'

'But how...?'

'Look, let's just get out of here before they change their minds. I'll tell you in the car, I've hired a car for a day or two.'

I had another Greek written paper I knew nothing about shoved across the desk by the duty officer. 'You should have brought Mabel,' I said. 'She could have translated this.'

'Would it have made any difference?' said Madge. 'You'd still have to sign it.'

'Probably not. Where is she anyway?'

'Look, what do you want, a welcoming party? You were an idiot. Mabel is sunning herself by the pool. She was a little nervous about visiting a jailhouse. Why the hell didn't you tell us about this stupid little escapade?'

'You'd have only talked me out of it.'

'You got that right.'

I signed the paper and the duty officer opened a drawer. He handed me back my camera. It was empty of course and we left.

Outside was parked a similar Seat car to the one I hired and we were off, soon out of Corfu Town and down scenic roads with rustic farmsteads and dusty olive and lemon groves on a beautiful evening promising a beautiful sunset and me feeling more relief than a squirt of haemorrhoid cream.

'So, if not bail, how did you swing it?' I asked.

'I bribed him,' said Madge. 'Castellanos has a price apparently, and you were in for a long time otherwise.'

'I suppose you learnt all about him from Christos?'

'That's right. Once we heard you were banged up, Christos told me all about Castellanos' free lunches. That spawned the idea for bribery.'

'That was risky,' I said

'Not if you wave enough dough under his nose. Anyway, we didn't go to him, he came sniffing around the hotel after, telling us all about your little night caper, saying you wouldn't see the light of day for months unless "someone was of a benevolent heart." His words exactly. Didn't need any translation, that one. Bent copper indeed, as Christos says. He even stayed for another free lunch and then he was snooping around the rooms again according to Elena. "Police work" he told her, no warrant or anything. But I didn't need to hear it from her. I could tell someone had been inside our rooms. He doesn't exactly try to hide it, that awful whiff of cigar. And

Mabel's room was the same. It's a travesty, an invasion of one's privacy. God knows what he's looking for now.'

'How much?' I asked.

'Two-hundred and fifty thousand Drachma.'

'For god's sake, woman, how can you afford that?'

'Don't panic,' said Madge. 'It's only about seven-hundred and fifty pounds in our money. My late husband was a surgeon. He left me quite a bundle when he passed away.'

'I'll pay you back, of course.'

'Bloody right you will. If I thought you'd been stitched up I wouldn't be bothered about it, but you've been a real naughty boy, I've heard. I mean, house breaking, then striking an officer of the law? What on earth were you thinking? You could have been banged up for years for the assault alone. Get your story, write it, publish and I'll have some of those royalties, thank you very much.'

'You won't have to wait that long. I'm not exactly broke,' I said.

I shut up for a while and just enjoyed the dusty ride with the car windows down blowing warm, clear air and not smelling sweat and staring at unpainted concrete. I'd forgotten how beautiful Corfu smelled outside of the town, a combination of wild herb, pine, hibiscus and citrus delicious enough to drink or spray your underarms with.

'You want to know what else Castellanos said?' said Madge.

'Go on.'

'He said you should pack up and go home on the next plane. I'm inclined to agree. You've ridden your luck with him. It might be good advice.'

'Well stuff that,' I said. 'I'm not forking out for an early flight. I've got the rest of the summer here. My agent wouldn't like it. It was his idea, to recuperate my writing skills, a little rest and...'

'Relaxation?' said Madge. 'Look, Angelo, let's just get you

back to the Aeres. Everyone's been worried about you. Relax a day or two and consider Castellanos' suggestion, then maybe book your passage home. And that's from me, not just Castellanos. I admit you've got grit for all your stupidity, but you lost. You must by now have at least the seeds of a novel from all this. Take it at that and quit while the going's good.'

'Maybe I want more than a story,' I mumbled.

'Anyway, you want to hear the good news?'

'Is there any?'

'Hector Thanos doesn't want to bring charges.'

'Ha! That proves his guilt,' I said. 'He doesn't want anything that draws attention to him.'

'For god's sake, Angelo, don't you get it? If Thanos wanted to bring charges there would be nothing either of us could do. Castellanos' hands would be tied and he'd have to charge you. No amount of bribery would have stopped you doing a long stretch in the slammer. But no, Thanos didn't want that. Apparently, he admires you.'

'What?'

'That's right,' said Madge. 'Castellanos told me Thanos admires you. That's the real reason you're free. Unfortunately Castellanos never mentioned that fact until I'd paid him off, the thieving scumbag. You were going free whether I bribed him or not. Bent copper is right; he's the very definition of it. Anyway, then he told me all about what Thanos said. Thanos knew it could only have been you, even before he found your boot and the escape rope. He thinks you're quite clever and a true adventurer. He actually likes you. He even quoted from that song: "Mad Dogs and Englishmen." Castellanos, however thinks you're "kefali peos."'

'What does that mean?'

'Mabel translated it for me. It means head penis. He thinks you're a dickhead. Something we agree on.'

'Charming.'

We arrived back at the Aeres at dusk to a more than warm welcome, lots of hugs and piles of food and wine I'd previously been dismissive of but now went down like ambrosia. I ate ravenously on moussaka, chips, green beans from the garden and red wine and crème caramel in an empty dining room, attempting to answer every question between mouthfuls. They didn't know about my night encounter with Charlie yet and I hadn't the energy to explain it. It seemed Castellanos hadn't mentioned him on his visit to the Aeres to gloat about my imprisonment and swindle Madge out of a bribe. I wondered if Castellanos even knew about Charlie. I wondered if Thanos would notice any change in Charlie. I doubted it. He'd been playful as a kitten with my rope.

The remaining guests had disappeared earlier into Gouvia for their nightly beers and Greek table dancing in the nearby taverns. I could hear them, the laughter and music drifted along the swaying curtains. Gouvia sounded pleasantly normal once again.

Madge and Mabel wanted to take me out on the town to celebrate straight after the meal, but I felt a sudden fatigue that threatened to overwhelm me and a need to get clean. I went upstairs for a shower, a long cool one. I hadn't had one for three nights and wanted to wash more than dirt away. I wanted to wash away the whole stinking experience, the prison with its poor souls, the depressing walls of bare concrete and most of all I wanted to see Castellanos swirling down the plughole.

I dried, put on clean boxers, a lathering of Deet and slept like a Deet covered log.

18.

In the morning I could see things had been moved about in my room. Castellanos had been snooping around the rooms during my detainment, like Madge had said, but I didn't care right then. I'd slept well, awoke late but refreshed and missed breakfast, but that didn't matter to Elena, who served me fresh croissants and coffee in an empty dining room.

I wanted a swim and a sun lounge and a little time to get things right in my head. I went back upstairs, got my trunks on, slipped my shorts over, grabbed sunglasses, tan oil, a towel and hit the pool.

On the way outside, Christos put his arm around my shoulder. 'You should have let me help. Next time you let me help, okay?'

'Okay,' I said. We shook on it. 'But you would still be in jail if you helped. Only the mercy of Thanos means I'm out.'

'Maybe,' said Christos. 'But I wouldn't be as stupid to leave my shoe and a rope behind. I would have made sure this didn't happen. Also you owe me one anchor, one length of tow-rope and one beef joint and an explanation of what you were doing with it. Okay?'

'I'm not even sure of that myself, Christos.'

Christos knew most of the story, at least that version received from the ladies who'd got Castellanos' version of it. I explained how I lost the anchor and rope first. Then I told him about the beef and Charlie. He'd heard about Charlie from Madge and Mabel and had suspected the joint was something to do with it. I explained it to him and he had a good laugh. I agreed a price for the lost items, cashed some traveller's cheques and paid him off.

'Tranquilizer gun next time,' said Christos.

'You can get me one?'

'Don't be stupid, Mr. Fox. Only in one of your books, Mr. Fox. Only in one of your books.'

Madge and Mabel were already by the pool laid out on Union Jack towels on loungers and drinking sangria.

'Well, well, well, Mabel,' said Madge. 'Look who it is, if it isn't Peter Scott himself.'

'I don't know who that is,' I said, 'but I don't think I'm going to like the explanation.'

'Peter Scott, the famous cat burglar.'

'The famous cat burglar,' repeated Mabel. 'He once stole a necklace worth two-hundred thousand pounds from Sophia Loren, you know.'

'And other stuff,' said Madge. 'I think he's in jail now.'

'You sure you don't want to bail him out?' I said.

'Now, now, don't be like that or I'll ask Castellanos for my money back.'

'Sorry. He'd probably give it you, just to see me sweat it out in jail if he had it his own way. Just shows how corrupt he is and in Thanos' palm.'

'Come and sit a while and have a sangria with us,' said Mabel. 'They make a rather lovely one at the bar here. They don't skimp on the brandy and red wine.'

I took a swim first. I walked to the deep end of the pool, stripped to my trunks, threw my shorts, shirt and sandals to the floor and dived in. It was beautiful, the cool, but not cold temperature of natural, filtered seawater. I'd always hated chlorinated water and this was as natural as can be without being in the actual sea. I didn't swim, I didn't have to. I turned on my back just gently waving my arms to stay afloat in its natural salt buoyancy looking up to spot the elusive, fluffy sheep-god clouds. I lay there for a long while and didn't care.

Madge and Mabel cared. I heard them through muffled, water-submerged ears. I raised my head. 'Well, are you going to tell us the rest of the story or what?' said Madge.

118

'Yes, tell us,' said Mabel. 'Get out and have a drink with us.'

I hauled myself out, towelled off and was given a sangria. They had a jug of it and a spare glass like they'd been expecting me. A beer would have gone down better, but being polite I pulled up a deckchair and spilled it. The story, not the sangria.

'Obviously Castellanos hasn't told you everything,' I said. 'Especially what he found on me.' I explained the finding of the three suspicious substances in Thanos' kitchen and how Castellanos rifled them off me along with my photos. 'He's guilty as hell of something, if not all the chaos in town. And I'm certain now he and Castellanos are behind Tobias being set up. And he'll know what Castellanos found on me. That's why he hasn't brought charges. He doesn't want anything coming out in court, whether I could prove it or not, which I can't now. So Thanos just allows me to go and anything I say is hearsay, the whisperings of a mad Englishman author with an overactive mind. That's the real reason he's let me go.'

'Go on,' said Madge.

'Yes, do go on,' repeated Mabel. 'This is turning out to be ever such a good story.'

'Only it isn't one,' I said. 'Thanos also doesn't know about my dealing with Charlie and neither does Castellanos.'

'Whatever do you mean?' said Madge. 'Surely it wasn't roaming about free at night?'

'I'm sure I explained this already. Charlie is like Thanos' guard dog. I apologise, by the way.'

'For what?' said Mabel.

'I'm afraid I duped you both,' I said. 'The sodium amytal capsules. I didn't take them for any insomnia. I saved them to try and drug Charlie.'

'Oh, what a ridiculous, hair-brained scheme,' said Madge. 'No wonder you didn't tell us. Did you really come up with that or are you fantasising your novel again?'

'It's all true,' I said. I could feel myself blushing with embarrassment. 'Friendly as Charlie was, he was still a real danger. I had to find a way of neutralising him for the night.'

I explained the whole idea, how I talked Christos into supplying me with the tools and the joint of beef I later stuffed with Mabel's sleep medication. 'I'm sorry I wasn't upfront with the truth, but I really had to do this on my own, my way. Only it didn't work.'

'What didn't?' said Mabel.

'The capsules,' I said. 'They didn't knock him out. I considered it very carefully, even asking my agent about the weight of an adult cheetah and working out what I thought would be a safe overdose to knock him completely without harming him. But they didn't work. As soon as I got back to the rope he was there. Thank god he remembered me. He was quite playful and happy and purring. I think he was thanking me for the meat. But they didn't work. He was as spritely as ever. I'm sorry; you must think I'm awfully deceitful.'

'No, I don't think that,' said Madge. 'I understand. I'm sure Mabel wouldn't have given you them if we'd known the truth.'

'I wouldn't have given you them,' repeated Mabel.

'I just think you don't know anything about cats,' said Madge.

'What do you mean?' I asked.

'Oh, for heaven's sake, Angelo' said Madge. 'It's obvious you've never owned a cat. Your Charlie cheetah just spat the damn capsules out. That's why it was still awake.'

'Sorry? I don't get it. I embedded them well into the joint.'

'You could have embedded them in its ass, it would still have avoided them. It's what cats do. Tell him, Mabel. Mabel has cats.'

'I have cats,' said Mabel. 'Tigger and Fusty. Two lovely toms that get on ever so well. But it's true what Madge says. Cats instinctively know when you've slipped something foreign into their food. If you've ever tried to give a cat a worm tablet, you'd know. You can stuff a worm tablet in the middle of a whole can of Kit-e-Kat and the cat will scoff the whole can, leaving the tablet behind in its dish. They just know how to avoid it. That's why they have nine lives. They're very clever like that. They know when something's not right.'

'So how do you worm your cats?' I asked.

'I just pick the cat up on my knee, lay him back in my arms and prise his mouth open and pop the tablet into the back of his throat and hold his mouth shut until he has no other option but to swallow. Tigger gets his first because if he sees Fusty getting one he runs and hides away, he knows what's coming, but Fusty isn't too fussy and doesn't struggle too much.'

'Great. I'll try that next time I meet a cheetah that needs worming.'

The rest of the story flowed like the sangria, sounding more surreal as it went, like listening to a drunkard at a bar telling his life story, interesting but often unbelievable. I wasn't even sure I believed it myself; it seemed that preposterous, if it wasn't for the two days in jail reality wakeup.

When I'd finished, Madge and Mabel were silent for a while. Madge spoke first: 'Really, Angelo? The cheetah was playing with the rope like a kitten plays with a ball of string? I trust you're not elaborating now. I know it was a brave, but totally stupid thing to do, but are you sure this isn't your writer's mind kicking in and you're not tagging things on to impress us?' She sat up, lathered on some more tanning oil, took another sip of sangria and lay down.

'I'm not tagging on anything,' I said. 'This is exactly how it happened.'

'Oh, I suppose so. We believe you, don't we, Mabel?'

'Of course we believe you,' said Mabel.

'To be honest, Angelo,' said Madge, 'if it was anyone else

I'd say they were a fibber, a Walter Mitty, even a liar-liar, pants-on-fire.'

Mabel tittered along: 'Liar-liar, pants-on-fire, tee hee.'

'Pants on fire,' Mabel repeated. She wasn't tittering.

'Enough, Mabel,' said Madge. 'We get it already.'

Mabel suddenly sat bolt upright, her sunglasses slipping from her face into the sangria jug. She pointed to the end of the pool. 'Pants on fire!' she shrieked.

Madge followed, sitting up so rapidly she upset the lounger and spilled onto the pool tiles.

I stared in disbelief. My shorts, still by the deep end, spluttered and popped like someone had stuffed firecrackers inside. I ran to the end and kicked them into the pool. If anything that made it worse. They floated and expanded, little shots of white hot sparks emitted, sounding like a popcorn maker with each bang and traces of white smoke floating up from the pool.

Pants on fire.

19.

Christos was fishing my shorts out of the pool with one of those long pole nets used to scoop out cigarette butts, leaves, palm seeds and once even an unwrapped Cadbury's picnic bar. He told me the bar was likely a prank by someone from the Club 18-30 and it worked.

Christos had just tipped the shorts out onto the poolside when Castellanos pulled into the hotel drive. He'd missed the drama and my ruined shorts had stopped smoking. He didn't get out of the car, but sat there puffing on his cigar and staring. I thought for a moment that Castellanos was responsible for my shorts. But I hadn't left them anywhere he could have rigged them up with bangers or whatever. He'd been in my room while I was in jail, but I had my shorts with me inside there. After a few minutes he leant his elbow out, stared at me and tapped his watch with a finger. Then he backed out and drove off. This was his way of telling me it was time to leave. He was anxious for me to leave Corfu. Why?

The other why was why did my pants catch fire? The answer came with the evening meal in the form of a young lad still at school when he wasn't working in the hotel.

Young Philo came to our table clutching a school exercise book and sat himself down. 'Mr. Fox? I think I might know why your shorts were on fire.'

I was puzzled. I thought at first the lad was about to confess to a prank, that he had stuffed something inside my shorts while I was floating in the pool half asleep. He opened the exercise book to a page with diagrams and formulas. 'There are only two things that can do this when they meet water,' Philo said. 'We learned this in science lesson last year.'

'Whatever is it?' said Madge.

'Our teacher did this experiment.' Philo pointed to the

diagram. 'He dropped a piece of sodium into a jar of water and 'bang!' It did exactly what your pants did, Mr. Fox. We did another experiment with potassium and that did the same. I think you had sodium or potassium in your pants.'

I sat back in my chair, astounded at this suggestion. 'But...but...I didn't have anything in my pants...wait a minute. Tell me something, Philo. What does this 'sodium or potassium' look like?'

'Like...like steel, or some other metal,' said Philo. 'Sodium looks like metal. Our science teacher said it was a metal. It's in group one on the periodic table. It's an element. When you drop it in water it makes hydrogen and sodium hydroxide. The bang is when the hydrogen explodes. It won't have done any harm to the pool water.'

'So...explain how your teacher conducted the experiment. Where was this sodium before he put it in the water?'

'In another jar. A jar of oil.'

I stared at Madge and Mabel. They stared back.

Elena came to the table with our desserts. 'Philo, stop annoying the guests, go help Christos in the kitchen, there is still work to do.'

'Sorry,' said Philo. 'I just thought it might be something like we learned about.' He got up to go.

I grabbed him by the arm. 'No...no, wait Philo,' I said. 'Sit down and tell me more about sodium or potassium. It was in oil, you say. What sort of oil, do you know?'

'Oryctellaio,' said Philo. 'That's what our teacher said. It stops the sodium from, from...reacting. It keeps it safe from water.'

'What is that, oryctellaio?'

'Mineral oil,' said Mabel. 'It means mineral oil. I suppose something like you oil squeaky hinges with.'

I think I sat with my jaw dropped like a doped psychiatric patient while time seemed to stop. 'Mineral oil...metal...mineral oil.' It hit me as hard as a Castellanos back-hander. 'The phial! The other phial! The phial in my slip pocket. Castellanos must have missed it. I assumed he'd emptied my pockets. I missed it. I never realised it must have still been there all the time. Damn these baggy pants and secret pockets! The third phial was still on me all this time and I never noticed. That's what it must have been! Sodium! Or potassium! Sodium in mineral oil! Potassium in mineral oil, it doesn't matter which, but it must have been one or the other.'

'So, how did it set off banging and burning?' said Madge.

'It must have leaked. The oil must have leaked out and my shorts lying on the wet poolside must have set it off! Philo, you're a genius, I could kiss you!'

So I kissed him. I grabbed his face between my hands and planted a big one on his forehead. Then I emptied my wallet of a few remaining drachmas and shoved them in his hands. Philo looked around furtively and shoved the notes into his exercise book, quickly shut it and scarpered off to help out in the kitchen.

I was elated. So elated I found myself tapping out a tuneless tune on my plate making the blancmange wobble like a belly dancer.

'There's just one small problem,' said Madge. 'The last bit of evidence you had against Thanos just went up in smoke.'

'I realise that,' I said. 'But it does show that Thanos is the main suspect behind events in Gouvia. Thanos also won't realise that I took some of his sodium as Castellanos didn't find it on me. I've kept the shorts for now, they could still be evidence.'

'But what could you possibly do with it?' said Madge. 'You're stuck on an island with a corrupt police chief. What's your plan? Who are you going to turn to?'

'The newspapers,' I said. 'I'll explain everything to my agent, get him to put me in contact with one and...'

'And get yourself sued for libel, that's what. You have no proof, Angelo. It'll be your word against a powerful property developer and the island's police department. You might as well go home, like Castellanos suggested.'

'Perhaps,' I said. 'But I don't like being bullied. There's more to this and I'm now almost certain an innocent young man is in jail. I still have some time here, maybe I'll just keep out of Castellanos' way until I think of something.'

We were silent for a while as we finished dessert. My mind ticked as a grandfather clock ticks – slowly, progressively, getting towards that inevitable strike of gong that supports an answer one is striving to solve. I was puzzling over what Thanos could possibly do with sodium or potassium other than leaking time bombs in people's pants. Then the mind-clock struck just as Philo came to the table clearing plates and thanking me for the generous tip and if I wanted to know anything else about chemistry. I did.

I sat him back down. 'You say mineral oil keeps the sodium inactive, correct?'

'Yes,' said Philo. 'Water can't get to it in the oil, just like oil stops metal going rusty. It stops oxygen getting to it.'

'Tell me something, Philo. Would sodium or potassium react with petrol, like if it was put into a petrol tank...in a car, for example?'

'What are you getting at, Angelo?' said Madge.

'Trust me, I'm working on a theory,' I said.

'I don't think so,' said Philo. 'You can keep the sodium in organic compounds such as kerosene, oils and I suppose gasoline as well. Organic compounds have a strong covalent bond which is very difficult to break, so sodium is kept in kerosene oils, which is similar in structure to gasoline...I mean petrol.'

I was deflated. My theory had just gone up in smoke like my pants. 'You're very clever, Philo and you'll go a long way, especially if you take up a science degree. That's all for now, thank you. I suppose you should get back to work before Elena scolds us both.'

'What on earth was all that about?' asked Madge.

Philo swung round in his chair to get up. Then he said: 'Until it came into the carburettor.'

I grabbed his arm again. 'Wait. What? What about the carburettor, Philo? Then what would happen?'

'If the sodium was moving around in the petrol and was drawn into contact with air in the carburettor, then yes...it would explode, first the hydrogen, then it would ignite the petrol.'

'And could that happen?'

'I suppose so. Sodium is light. It floats in the oil, so...'

'So small granules of it could float in petrol in a tank and when the tank is agitated by an engine running those small granules could be drawn into the carburettor of the boat...I mean the engine. And someone could say, drop some in say a tank of water, perhaps. Near some gas bottles near a crowd, for example and... '

Philo was staring at me with wide eyes. I was gripping his arm a little too hard.

Madge grasped my hand and gently removed it from Philo. 'That's all for now, Philo,' she said.

Philo left, rubbing his arm and Madge scolded me. 'What was all that about? You were scaring him. I see exactly what you're driving at, that boat out on the bay that caught fire, maybe even something to do with the rally. But there's still nothing you can do about it. And have you asked yourself why you think Thanos might be behind all this? What's the motive? Not only have you no evidence, you have no motive. What are you going to tell these "newspapers?"'

'What would Jimmy Finn do?' said Mabel.

'Shut up, Mabel,' said Madge. 'This is not the time or place for a Jimmy Finn. This has gotten beyond seriousness. Go home, Angelo. Get your reporter, tell him what you know and what you suspect, but don't dress it up as fact. If they're interested, let them do the digging. They have a certain protection in journalism, you don't. And they have a duty to protect the anonymity of their sources. Whatever you do, don't go trying to sell them a "story." That could land you in court.'

'But what if they don't listen to him?' said Mabel.

'Oh, I think they will,' said Madge. 'They already know about Dave Barton's poisoning back home. God knows how that's affecting holiday sales to Gouvia. And no doubt they'll have heard about the explosion at the rally by now, so they could be interested if you tell them what you found. You have no evidence, of course, but it's unlikely they'll dismiss someone with a high public profile such as yourself as a liar. Think about it.'

Madge took my hand gently across the table and patted it.

Mabel put her hand on top of Madge's and gently patted them both. 'Think about it,' she repeated, then finished her blancmange.

Madge finished her blancmange.

I didn't finish my blancmange.

I really wanted crème caramel.

20.

We found ourselves at 'Spyros' on the Sand' after sunset where the moths commit suicide in oil lamps on bamboo stakes stabbed haphazardly along the shore. I sat on a cane chair by the water's edge where the sea lapped my bare feet and the flickering light was just enough to see what I was drinking.

Mabel skipped along the shore holding her dress up and kicking the water as she went. She said she'd brought her swinger with her.

'What's his name?' I said.

'No silly, my camera. My Polaroid Swinger. It takes instant photos, you know. You have to shake them dry when they pop out. Aren't modern inventions wonderful?'

'I know how they work.'

She skipped back up the beach to the bar where Madge was struggling to carry two cocktails and a beach bag. They paddled a while, cocktails in hand. I sat watching out to the faint horizon and the faint light of a couple of fishing boats reflecting on a beautifully calm sea. Calm as my mind was at that moment, probably as calm as it had been since day three and Dave Barton's untimely death. I wanted it to stay that way. I felt calm and defeated. Madge was right and I was leaning towards surrender and going home.

Three cocktails later and the Swinger appeared from the beach bag. Madge and Mabel ran up and down the beach laughing and snapping and shaking prints like it was a new dance craze. Mabel snapped Madge, Madge snapped Mabel, Mabel snapped the barman with Madge, Madge snapped Mabel with the barman, the barman snapped Madge and Mabel and Mabel held the camera at arm's length and snapped the barman, Madge and herself all squashed together. She got all of herself and two halves of Madge and the barman in the frame.

'One day someone will invent an easier way of taking a photo of one's self,' said Mabel.

'You should patent the idea,' I said sarcastically. 'I'm sure it will catch on.'

'Oh, listen to old grumpy drawers,' said Madge.

'Grumpy drawers,' repeated Mabel. 'Here, I've one print left for old grumpy drawers.' She pranced in front of me, blocking the sedating view of floating lights on the sea and shoved the camera in my face, temporarily blinding me with the flash. 'Cheer up, Angelo, you'll be home soon.' Out popped the print and Mabel wafted it about like an oriental fan.

'And you'll have most of what you need for a new book,' said Madge. 'I can't wait to see how it ends.'

'I suppose so,' I said. 'There's nothing left I can do here, and with Castellanos on my tail to boot. I'll be glad to get back, but oh so regretful I couldn't do more.'

'Well remember my advice when you see your reporter. In the meantime let's just enjoy the time you have with us. We'll miss you, you know.'

'And here's a reminder of how happy you were,' said Mabel. She stopped fanning and looked at the print, then burst out laughing. 'This is so funny! Look, Madge!'

Madge took the photo and also burst into laughter. 'Now doesn't that just remind you of something?'

Madge handed me the print, a close-up of my grumpy, puzzled looking face that filled the frame. 'Now who does that remind you of?' she said.

'A constipated Robert Morley,' I said. 'Why? What relevance is it?'

'No, don't you see? I mean it's like Thanos, of course. The photo you took of him, I mean the one he accidently took of himself, that is. You know, the one of his whole perplexed face looking into the lens like a lost child. It's like you two could be crime buddies in a wanted poster.'

I jumped up from my chair. 'I quite forgot. Mabel, have you still got that photo?'

'Why, yes,' said Mabel. 'It's right here in my bag still.'

She got the photo out and handed it to me. I held it next to the one of me. 'This must be why Castellanos came back snooping. I think Thanos must have realised that there may be an image of him out and got Castellanos to search for it. It all makes sense now. I bet he even knew he'd accidentally taken a snap of himself, but daren't ask me to hand over the film as that would raise even more suspicion. He let me be released from jail so Castellanos could try and get it. He was hoping it was on my last roll of film he confiscated.'

I dried my feet, grabbed my shoes and made my way up the beach.

'Where are you going?' said Madge.

'To the hotel. There's a reason Thanos doesn't like being photographed, and somehow I'm going to find out why.'

When I got to the Aeres, Elena was waiting for me by the reception desk. 'He is upstairs now, snooping around again,' she said. 'I try to stop him, but he just says police business. Always police business, that's his excuse for pushing us around and being horrible to us and helping himself to our food and drinks.'

'Castellanos?'

'Yes, be careful, Mr. Fox, he is not in a good mood.'

Madge and Mabel had followed me to the hotel, arriving shortly after. I handed the photo of Thanos back to Mabel explaining the situation. 'Take it and get lost for a while. I'll come looking for you when he's gone.'

I was the one not in a good mood. I half expected Castellanos to be in my room and I was right. Deet sat in a corner on the only chair in the room. Castellanos sat with his half-ass on the Cezanne table. He looked relaxed but serious and he was fouling the air. Then he lit a cigar. He took a long draw on his gold-labelled corona and blew a plume of camel fart into the room. Mosquitoes headed to the corners. Cigars and sweaty cops have that same effect on me.

'Where is it?' Castellanos said. He picked up my photo envelope from the table, the prints I had developed in Corfu Town.

'What?' I said.

'You know what I mean. Your camera uses twenty-four shot film cassettes. I know this from the film I confiscated.' He held the prints envelope up by his ear, like it was going to tell him what to say next. 'There are twenty-three prints here – one missing. I know this from the negatives I counted. Twenty-four negatives, but only twenty-three prints.'

'Well then, you don't need the print. If you're so fond of him get another one developed and pin him up on your wall. I binned that one, it was embarrassing. Not exactly a holiday snap you'd want to show your friends.'

'So, you know who I am talking about.' Castellanos snapped his fingers and Deet stood up. 'Search him.'

Deet frisked me like he'd learned how from a 1950s film noir cop movie, patting me up and down the shorts and shirt with my hands raised all in about five seconds.

Castellanos didn't look amused. 'Take your shorts off and throw them on the bed.'

I dropped them. I threw them on the bed and Deet rifled through them, turning out the pockets, the wallet, stood back and shrugged his shoulders.

'Now the underpants,' said Castellanos.

I dropped the underpants around my ankles. 'You really still want the photo if it's been stuck to my balls? I told you I disposed of it. I tore it up and threw it away. It'll be a piece of rat-chewed pulp in Trashtown by now. I take it you've already searched the room. Whatever interest it is to you, I can't imagine, but it's gone. I can assure you of that.'

Castellanos slid his ass off the table abruptly. It came out from under him with a scrape and a skid along the tile floor like he'd farted it out. He marched up to me and poked a finger the colour of a finny-haddock into my neck. 'I want you gone. Three days and I arrest you for assault. Damn what Hector Thanos says.'

They left with a slam of the door, taking my only remaining holiday photos.

The mosquitoes were happy again.

I dressed, waited half an hour then slipped quietly downstairs to speak to Elena. 'I want you to do something for me,' I said. 'You allowed me into the hotel garden before to be alone, to do some writing in peace. My two friends, the ladies Mabel and Madge will be coming back to the hotel later. I want you to allow them back in from the garden, if that's alright, through the kitchen.'

'Yes, but of course,' said Elena. 'This is to do with Castellanos, I am sure.'

'It is. Castellanos is harassing me. He thinks I have something he wants and I've no doubt he'll want to harass my two friends when they return later tonight. Mabel will have something for you. I want you to lock it up in the hotel safe.'

'I will leave the kitchen door unlocked for them and wait,' said Elena. 'Be sure they are very quiet, please. I know the ladies like to have a drink, but no giggling please, especially if it's late. I do this for Jimmy Finn.'

'Oh, they'll be quiet alright, I'll see to it. I don't want them making noise any more than you or the remaining guests here do. And I'm not Jimmy Finn. I can't imagine who told you that.' I could, of course.

Castellanos was waiting alright. He was in an unmarked car on the road about twenty yards from the hotel drive. A cursory eyeball glance was all it took. Unmistakable. A dirty fat cigar stuck out from a larger than life dirty black moustache sat on a round face behind the wheel of the only car on the road and a dumb-as-fuck looking Deet in the passenger seat. Hardly anyone in Gouvia owned cars. He was conspicuous by his presence. He wasn't even trying to be covert. I walked by and didn't acknowledge him. Shortly after I passed I heard the car start and turn around in the road. Slowly it tailed me, keeping at my pace. I stopped and pretended to adjust my sandal. The car stopped. I didn't turn around. I just ignored him and carried on. I passed by Niko's bar and noticed the ladies weren't there, so I stopped and ordered a beer. Castellanos passed by, turned his car around and parked a short way down the road.

I had a couple of drinks and a chinwag with Niko. We talked a while about recent events in Gouvia and the fact that tourists had once again come out to drink and dine. More importantly to him was that they were back in his bar, wary, but still enjoying themselves. I wasn't, but pretended to be. I disclosed to Niko that Castellanos was tailing me. He didn't know about my incarceration and release, so I told him, but not the details. I lied and said that I got into an argument with Castellanos at the Aeres, insulted him and that my friend Madge had posted bail. I'm not sure if he bought it, but explaining Hector Thanos was out of the question and would take all night. I didn't have all night. I needed to find Madge and Mabel as soon as I could before Castellanos got bored of watching me and started looking for them himself.

'This does not surprise me,' Niko said. 'Castellanos is a bully and likes to intimidate people. He is bothered that you have been released and can't do anything about it. He is trying to intimidate you, to get you to do something that will give him an excuse to arrest you again. He is not well liked in Gouvia, but the people are afraid of him, so they go about their business and serve him when he wants to hustle us. It is best to keep out of his way.'

Niko had a plan.

Another beer and I went to the men's room and climbed out the back window into Niko's private garden in the rear. Following his instruction, I hopped over the stone wall at the end and followed it right to a path that led to the road some way behind Castellanos' car. I slipped across in the faint light between street-lamps to another side road that led through a pine-wooded glade to another path that weaved between hotels and onto the path leading down to Spyros' on the Sand. As I expected, Madge and Mabel were there.

I explained the situation. 'That photo of Thanos is the only evidence I have left that I met up with him. It may be a long shot, but I have an idea.'

'Whatever is it?' said Madge.

'You'll see. It may be something of nothing, but it's my last punt at getting to the truth. Whatever happens, Castellanos must not get hold of that photo. There's a reason he's looking for it. I'm beginning to believe that's the real reason Thanos didn't file charges against me. Because Castellanos hasn't found the photo, Thanos wanted me out of custody so that Castellanos can follow me to try and find it. That's all I'm saying for now.'

'Oh dear,' said Mabel. 'I hope this isn't going to get you arrested again.'

'No, it's not,' I said. 'When you get into the hotel, Elena will be waiting for you in the kitchen. Give her the photo for safe-keeping.'

We had a last drink and left via the back lanes to the main road outside the orchard garden of the Aeres. Madge and Mabel slipped silently through the gap between the palm tree and hibiscus as they had before on the day they disturbed my peace. I went round to the road at the front of the hotel and walked on as though I'd done nothing more than go out for a quiet drink. Castellanos' car was there, back in its original place. I passed by, expecting him to jump out and question me. He didn't. I reckon he must be thinking he'd blinked and missed me leaving Niko's, or maybe he'd given way to temptation, left his vigil and helped himself to a free drink in one of the bars. Maybe it was in Niko's. Maybe he went for a piss and found the back window open.

I didn't care, he let me walk by. He didn't want me now. Derek Plumpton had no film for him and Jimmy Finn had eluded him. Angelo Fox had outfoxed him.

He was waiting for Madge and Mabel.

Sucker.

21.

In the morning Castellanos was once again parked up along the road not far from the hotel drive. I didn't let him see me. I sneaked out to the pool, around to the far side and peered through some hedging. Maybe he'd stayed there all night. I didn't care right then. He didn't try the one stupid thing I worried he might try. I did think that Castellanos might even try some sort of early hour raid on the hotel to try and get the photo. But that would have been massively stupid even for him. Without any warrants and no conceivable crime having been committed to get one, he'd be acting alone and illegally. A lot of what Castellanos was getting away with was illegal – even by Greek law, but a shed load of complaints from the guests to the holiday company would no doubt attract the attention of the British Consulate in Corfu and questions would be asked. His stupid little free meals and drinks racket would be exposed. Even someone as brash or dumb as Castellanos wouldn't risk that.

If only the photo of Thanos had occurred to me before the previous night I would have got more copies. But now Castellanos had the negatives. The camera shop in Corfu could maybe make a copy from the print, but in how long? And a print copy rather than a negative processed one loses resolution. Would it still be of any use to my intended recipient? And now I was a watched man anyway. I wasn't going anywhere.

I had initially considered posting the photo to my agent and getting him to pass it along to my police friend Dreyfus. Adam Dreyfus, who'd kindly helped me in previous crime novel research was now a semi-retired detective, but still had access to international crime departments and files. In the past he'd worked on cases of criminals absconding abroad and bringing them home. But I had three days left and no doubt that Castellanos would fill out his threat and the postal service was way too slow. And I had no intention of leaving Corfu yet, not until I found out more. And not while a man I knew was innocent was still in prison. I knew if I posted it I'd be at least a week into my re-incarceration before Dreyfus even got the photo and I wouldn't even know about it if he replied and I also thought he might not want to help a guy who'd got himself arrested. I doubted he'd know about the first, but two arrests and I'd be on my own. He was a copper – ex or not – still a copper after all, not a solicitor. And coppers don't like to be seen helping cons. Even crime writer ones.

But the gods, it seemed (fluffy sheep ones, at that) were in my favour, although I couldn't see it at first. I returned to the dining room where breakfast was just being served, had my coffee and cake and confided in the ladies.

'I don't know what to do,' I said.

'Well, if you weren't being so furtive and acting like Jimmy Finn, we might be able to help,' said Madge.

'Yes,' said Mabel. 'Acting just like Jimmy Finn. Tell us what's happening.'

'I must get the photo of Thanos to someone I know in the UK. I know I said it's a long shot, but I need to find out more about Hector Thanos and why Castellanos is so desperate for that photo of him. I can't post it, it'll take days to get there and Castellanos is about to arrest me if I stay beyond his deadline. And he's watching my every move. Given time he could even get a new warrant out and access to the hotel safe. Elena's holding the photo there for me.'

'Oh dear,' said Madge. 'And you call yourself a crime writer?'

'What's that supposed to mean?'

'Well, look around you. Notice anything different today?'

I looked around the dining room. Same as usual, fewer

guests, gentle breeze through the long curtains that colour-matched Mabel's dress, coffee, croissants and an overhead fan that creaked and fought a losing battle with the breeze. 'I don't get it?' I said.

'The guests,' said Madge. 'It's Saturday. Haven't you seen the suitcases?'

'It's change-over day today,' said Mabel. 'The package holiday guests are going home today and new guests will be coming to the hotel tonight. We've seen two changes of guests so far this stay. They're all such lovely people too...except for that awful Mr. Barton. Still though, he didn't deserve what happened to him.'

'What are you trying to say?' I said.

'Well, it's quite simple,' said Madge. 'Ask one of the departing guests to deliver the photo for you. Put it in an envelope with an address and ask kindly. Be quick though, the airport coach will be coming for them in about an hour.'

'Brilliant!' I said. 'But what do I say? I can hardly tell whoever accepts it the truth, especially if any of them know about my arrest.'

'Nobody has mentioned your arrest,' said Mabel. 'We've said nothing to anyone about that. It might reflect badly on the hotel. And Elena would certainly say nothing. Things have been troubling enough, but that might lose her more guests. So, I doubt anyone other than us know about it.'

'Tell them anything you like,' said Madge. 'Just say it's an important document that can't wait.'

'It's risky,' I said. 'I even thought about sneaking out myself and heading for the airport in hope of catching an unreserved seat on the next flight, but I think Castellanos will have someone looking out for me even if I got past him.'

'He will,' said Mabel. 'We had a walk before breakfast. He's got that one you call Deet posted on the road outside the kitchen garden. He's watching alright.'

'Got a better idea?' said Madge.

'No,' I said. 'But Castellanos will guess that I might try something like that. Even though I doubt he'll search everyone, I've no doubt that if he suspects anyone of carrying for me, he'll question them. And that's going to spook whoever it is.'

'Of course it will, but only if he thinks of it. But it's your only chance. Even if you manage to stay for your full term here and manage to stay out of his way, he'll get you at the airport, or on the way to it. There's a reason they're both hanging out there outside. And he'll have other spies you don't even know about yet, if he really wants that photo. It's either get one of the homebound guests to be your courier, or forget the whole thing, tear up the photo and go home. The latter would be my suggestion. You've risked too much already. It's time to stop being Jimmy Finn for once.'

I stood up sharply at that. 'Just remember it was you that wanted me to do a Jimmy Finn in the first place.'

I marched into the kitchen and found Elena. I asked for the photo and a manila envelope, got them both and retreated to my room. I scribbled a quick letter, signed it, sealed it with the photo and addressed it and went quickly back downstairs.

I marched into the dining room where most of the remaining guests were either finishing breakfast or drifting into the reception area to await the airport transfer. I cleared my throat. Then I cleared it again, louder this time.

'Excuse me,' I started. I started with an apology and got looks like I'd lost something. 'Excuse me,' I said again. 'May I have everyone's attention for just a moment or two?'

I had everyone's attention. I hadn't prepared a speech and got momentarily stuck. 'May I just say...on behalf of the Aeres...and the wonderful Elena and the boys...a big thank you for having faith and not running off after some most unfortunate events. That means a lot to the family...and to me...and I hope you'll all return in the future.

'In the meantime, I have a small request, just a little favour that I'd like someone to fulfil for me. I have a very important document here that I'd quite forgotten to post before coming out here and I didn't realise it was still in my belongings...at the bottom of my suitcase, actually. Silly me, I don't know how I could have missed it.'

'What is it?' someone asked.

'Err...well...' I hadn't thought it through.

Mabel read my dilemma. 'It's a manuscript,' she said.

I stood there with my skinny envelope looking at a dozen puzzled faces. I heard Mabel grunt as Madge nudged her. 'Actually, it is in a sort of way. It's some corrections to a manuscript I've already submitted to an agent. The thing is the book is due to go to the publishing editor's desk and I made some changes. Then I forgot to post them. This is it in my hand. Some simple, but important modifications I've noted that must reach the agent by Monday. The postal service won't be quick enough; it'll be unlikely to leave the island before then. I need someone to deliver it for me. Anyone?'

A dozen puzzled faces stared at me and each other.

'Where are you all headed to?' I asked.

Five hands went up.

'We're Manchester airport bound,' said a young lady. I recognised the girl who first spoke to me over breakfast after Barton's death.

'That's excellent,' I said. 'Manchester is where the agent is based.' I was lying. My agent was London based, but Dreyfus' private address was in Hyde, Manchester. That was how I addressed the envelope. 'Would you be so kind? I'll award you of course, for the inconvenience and the travel. It's very important to me, you know. I could look such a fool if these amendments aren't received.'

'Why don't you just phone the agent?' said the young lady. 'And read out the amendments to him?'

I was flustered again, but Madge spoke up before Mabel had chance to stick her foot in it. 'Well, he's tried that several times, but the phone service on the island is notoriously bad, isn't it, Angelo?'

'Notoriously bad,' I repeated.

'Notoriously bad,' Mabel repeat mumbled.

'You're that brash author who was so flippant about Mr. Barton's death,' said the young lady. 'You're Jimmy Finn, aren't you?'

'I'm not...Oh never mind, yes, that's me,' I said. 'And your name is?'

'Diane. And you were very rude that morning too. Very dismissive, just like Jimmy Finn. And then you moved tables the next day so you didn't have to sit next to us.'

'That's right,' said her companion. 'It's like you didn't like us or we smelled or something.'

'I once read a book of yours and thought it was okay,' said Diane. 'But do you always act like a prat, or do you have to practice?'

Madge and Mabel tittered. 'He always acts like Jimmy Finn,' said Madge. 'It's called 'getting into character' and we like him that way. Except when he becomes a grumpy old man.'

'He can be a grumpy old man at times,' said Mabel.

'Look, I'm sorry,' I said. 'They're right, sometimes I get into this persona of my character and I can't help it. I don't mean to offend. Heaven knows, it's got me into bother in the past. And as far as moving table goes, I needed to be alone, that's all. I needed to concentrate on my writing ideas. It's nothing personal; I treat everyone equally as disgracefully.'

'There you go again,' said Diane. 'Being so flippant.'

I looked around the room. 'Anyone? If anyone is willing to be a courier...I'll see that you're amply rewarded, of course.'

'Okay, I'll do it,' said Diane.

'Really?' I said.

'For an ample reward.'

'Of course, I just said that. What would you consider a fair recompense for your inconvenience?'

'Well...taxi fare from Hyde for a start,' said Diane.

'Taxi? Yes, it shall be done. I'll pay you now. I have Sterling and traveller's cheques in the hotel safe. How far will it be?'

'We live in Howarth, North Yorkshire. About fifty-five miles, I think.'

'I thought you said you lived in Manchester?' I said.

'I didn't say that. We are flying back to Manchester. And if we decide to deliver your envelope we'll miss our transfer bus to Howarth. So, taxi it is. Probably about thirty quid plus tip. Plus the cost we already paid out for the transfer bus. That was another twenty pounds. And a Courier charge. I think about fifty quid should cover that. Call it an 'inconvenience' charge. I mean you are an author after all. I can see these manuscript changes mean a lot to your next book. I'm sure that's small change by your royalties.'

'Done,' I said.

'And I want to be in your next book. And I don't mean as a credit on the inside cover. Make me a character. I've always wanted to be a villain, either in a Bond movie or a book. Make me a villain.'

'You already are.'

The transfer bus pulled into the hotel drive and I had to act. 'Deal,' I said. 'I'll write you in.'

'And use my real name?' said Diane.

'Yes, your real name...and a credit. And I'll include a footnote in the back about how highway robbers still exist.'

I handed her the envelope and withdrew all my available Sterling cash from the hotel safe and handed her that also, a hundred and fifty pounds in all. 'That should cover it, I hope. Just a couple of small favours I ask. The man's name is Dreyfus, it's on the envelope. I want you to hand it to him personally and mention my name, if he's home at the time. And can you please put the envelope in your suitcase?'

'Why, don't you trust me?'

'I trust you implicitly. But I don't trust bag snatchers and pickpockets. It's a precaution. It's copyrighted material and must not get into the wrong hands.'

And above all I don't trust Castellanos, I thought.

The tour guide was calling them and the driver had almost finished loading luggage into the hold by the time Diane had locked the envelope in and handed her suitcase to the guide. I breathed a sigh of relief. Then I breathed a gasp of dismay. The nightmare I dreaded most was unfolding. Castellanos was wandering his way down the drive, Deet alongside him and halting the guests from boarding.

I stood well back in the shadow of the reception area watching. He was questioning them. I couldn't hear what was said, but I guessed what it was about. The guests mostly shrugged their shoulders. Maybe Castellanos was as dumb as I suspected and was asking if anyone was carrying a 'photo' instead of an envelope or package.

Then, suddenly Diane looked at me. I doubted she could actually see me, just a dark figure in the shade, but she knew I was there. She looked frightened. Castellanos was talking to her. His back was towards me and I stepped into the light as she looked over his shoulder. I smiled and gave her the thumbs up as if all was normal. On the outside I was sweating. Inside I was praying and needing a toilet. She looked back at Castellanos. He was still talking. Maybe it was my imagination, but it seemed like he was spending more time on her. Then she shook her head and Castellanos moved onto the next guest. Diane quickly boarded, followed by her companion. Deet shrugged his shoulders and Castellanos threw his arms in the air as the last guest boarded. He was pretty dumb, but not dumb enough to delay the coach and strip everyone's bags and cases.

Diane neither waved nor smiled as the coach pulled out of the drive. She couldn't see me now stood back in the shade of the reception. I didn't want Castellanos to see me and get suspicious. I was also trying to make it look perfectly normal to Diane, like I'd gone back inside to finish breakfast. She had seemed rattled, and maybe that's why she never waved. I never did know the conversation that took place, but whatever it was, it seems the smell of cash and the lure of having fifteen minutes of fame at least had won over. And Castellanos had to accept that I must have destroyed the photo. He'd lost this round and I went to the bar and ordered a large stiff brandy and a jug of sangria for Madge and Mabel.

Then I paid a visit to the men's room.

22.

Two days left. Two days and I was certain Castellanos would carry out his threat. But I could go home now. It wouldn't matter if Castellanos stopped and searched me on the way. There was nothing to find. But something still nagged me inside and I still resented that Castellanos thought he had the right to end my stay on the island. In the letter I had asked Dreyfus to phone me if he found anything about Hector Thanos and if I left the island too soon I'd miss that call. So I waited.

All that day I never wandered from the hotel. I hung around, lounging by the pool with a drink and scribbling the odd line into my notebook. I wanted to start the new book. I wanted to know the ending first and I wanted the ending here in Corfu. I asked the Samaras family to be on the alert for a phone call. It didn't come, not that day nor the next. My time was up and I had to leave. I didn't want to. Something inside was holding me up, telling me I needed to wait a while. But time was frittering away and I knew Castellanos would be waiting for me to move. I had to be seen, suitcase in hand leaving the Aeres.

I was laid by the pool again, about to get up and pack for the airport in hope of catching either a cancellation or charter flight when Christos read my thoughts.

'You do not want to go, Mr. Fox,' he said. 'I can tell this.'

'Can you?' I said. 'Why do you think that is?'

Christos pulled up a plastic deck chair and sat by me. He looked up at the clear sky a while. 'Another beautiful day on Corfu. Such a shame to leave for your cold country now that summer is nearly ended. But that is not why you don't want to leave. You want to stay for justice. I know you are now thinking that Tobias is innocent and that he has been 'stitched up' by that bent copper and you feel you can't leave yet.'

'You're very astute, Christos. Almost psychic I'd say. I did find some evidence at the mansion that may have proven Tobias is innocent, but Castellanos took it. And I'd love to stay longer, at least until I got the phone call I'm waiting for. I have a friend in England who is trying to find out a little more about Hector Thanos for me. But the truth is Castellanos will arrest me if I stay any longer. He can do that, I did slap him after all and Hector Thanos is the only reason I'm not in jail right now. So, I think I'm going, today even.'

'You can hide,' said Christos. 'Hide until you find out what you need to know.'

'Where?' I said. 'Castellanos will most likely know if I haven't caught a flight home. He'll check at the airport, the passenger lists and all. He has the authority to do that. And if he finds out I haven't gone, he'll look for me. He'll check the guest lists of every hotel in Gouvia. Even if I give a false name, he'll describe me and threaten every hotelier here until they give me up. And if I'm at another hotel, I'll miss my phone call anyway.'

'I can hide you, Mr. Fox.'

'You, Christos?'

'Of course. I have a place. I have a property a few miles from here.'

'I thought you lived here, at the hotel?'

'Mostly,' said Christos. 'I told you about this once before. You said I was like a 'navvy,' because I have strong arms. In the summer, when the guests are here I live at the Aeres. But I have a place of my own. It's something Papa insisted on, that us boys should not rely on him and Mama forever. We should have property of our own, for when we meet our wives. Philo still lives with Mama, of course, until he finishes school. Papa left money, enough for us to start. I will be paying for my house for many years, but one day it will be mine, and of course, some very lucky woman.'

'I remember you saying, Christos. You are very lucky. You will make a good husband and one day a good father, I'm sure.'

'So, what do you say, Mr. Fox? Will you stay a little longer? If there is any chance of Tobias to prove his innocence, then I want you to stay and find out. Whatever you can do, I will help. I can show you my place. I said I will always help you, if you let me.'

'Castellanos will know I haven't left the island.'

'But he will never know where you are. And I will take a message from your friend and let you know that he has phoned. I will tell him to phone again at a later time and come and get you for the later time. Easy. And you will love my place, peace and quiet and finish your book.'

'So, what's the plan?' I asked.

I still had another month before my scheduled flight back home, but Castellanos had no regard for that. He was there on his deadline day, parked in his usual place not far from the hotel drive.

Christos' plan was cleverly simple. I packed all my stuff that morning, knowing Castellanos would inspect my vacant room after. I thought he would likely ask Elena for passports from the safe, so I took that as well. I felt guilty fibbing to Madge and Mabel, but I couldn't take the risk of Castellanos bullying and harassing them into the truth. I left the Aeres, carrying my suitcase and a parcel, walked out to the road, past a smiling Castellanos in his car and around the corner to the Corfu Town bus stop, where Deet sat upon a bench opposite. The bus pulled up, blocking Deet's view, Christos popped out of the hotel orchard hedge, took my suitcase, popped back into the hedge and disappeared. I hopped on the bus and disappeared from Gouvia.

About three miles away Castellanos watched as an old peasant man in ragged clothes in a tatty, wide-brimmed straw peasant's hat, carrying a burlap shoulder bag, stepped down from a bus at a dusty stop, hobbled across the road and disappeared down a lane at the side of a tavern. Decoy complete. I knew he would continue following the bus to Corfu Town and the airport and he did.

Sucker.

23.

Christos was waiting, hidden off the lane on the dirt track he'd described. He laughed as he saw me approach the Land Rover.

'How was the bus journey?' he said.

'I sat near the back,' I said. 'Fortunately no one was behind me. Swapping shorts for old pants was the trickiest part, but I don't think the driver realised, at least he never said anything as I stepped off.'

'And Castellanos?'

'He took off after the bus. He'll know, of course, that I've eluded him somewhere, but he won't know where exactly. Several other passengers alighted at stops before mine and there will be other stops further on before Corfu Town.'

'You play the part beautifully, Mr. Fox. Jimmy Finn would be proud.'

'Where on earth did you get these awful clothes?' I said.

'Hey!' said Christos. 'These are my own clothes when I'm doing work on my house. Such an insult!' He was still laughing as I climbed into the Rover. 'Your suitcase is in the back, you can change when we arrive.'

I stayed far longer than I had anticipated. Three days passed and I heard nothing, either from Dreyfus or Christos. Christos had catered for me well. There was ample food, no fridge but a cool cellar larder stocked with canned goods, some fresh vegetables, coffee and an earthenware crock with cheese, butter and bread. There was electricity wired to the lights only, a wood burning stove and no TV, radio or phone. Christos had promised to return on notice of Dreyfus' call and rightly pointed out that to keep leaving the hotel to check up on me would catch the attention of Castellanos, who no doubt would be on the lookout.

Christos showed me where everything was kept, lit a fire in the wood burner and made coffee before departing. He backed the Land Rover out and I was alone.

But I didn't mind. For the first time since arriving on Corfu, I was truly alone with my thoughts. I had a book to write, the idea, some rough notes. An ending was needed. And now I realised why something inside nagged me to stay that little bit longer than Castellanos' deadline. The ending. I unpacked my things, sat at the kitchen table with another coffee and started writing, assembling my notes into a coherent and sequential tale. Only it wasn't a tale. And I was waiting for that answer that decided if I needed to fictionalise the rest.

Christos' place wasn't bad at all. I had a kitchen with exposed beams, no ceiling and a stone tile roof that showed patches of daylight on the table and stone floor and a comfortable bed. The small hacienda-style was rustic, with part whitewashed exterior, exposed concrete and stone, and a gable-end that didn't quite reach the roofline. Stone piles, concrete mixer, spades and workmen's tools in a barrow inside the gable were testimony to Christos' hard off-season work. The rest was Corfu on a postcard, a rough gravel drive from the secluded lane to a bright blue painted door, a couple of lemon trees by the house, and a field on a gentle slope leading to a woodland of wild olive and pine trees swaying and casting shades of violet over grasses the colour of ochre and sienna.

The nights were a strange creature to me, strange birds and wildlife sounds crept in through the shutters, battened against the moths. I chose to work by oil lamp as an added measure against their curiosity, the odd one or two finding their way in between the cracks. Castellanos' face loomed out of the darkness when I retired. I kept imagining him outside on that first night. But I applied my mind to the writing, and Christos' assurance at my complete solitude saw him fade into the back of a cigar-smoked office miles away.

On the fourth day it came, but at what time I wasn't sure. It was late and I'd forgotten to wind my watch for several days and it stopped on the second day. I heard the crunch of gravel and familiar hum of the Land Rover.

'He will phone the Aeres again in two hours, Mr. Fox,' said Christos. 'I haven't seen Castellanos in two days, but that doesn't mean he isn't looking out for you.'

'You don't need to tell me the obvious, Christos,' I said. I took only the clothes I wore, hiding the rest of my belongings in a locked cupboard Christos had shown me in the cellar, in the event I had to return to my hideout. Entering Gouvia, I kept my head down should Castellanos be about. Christos drove the Rover straight into the garage and ensured the coast was clear. I sneaked into the kitchen via the garden door. The hotel was quiet, the evening meal had finished and guests had left for the taverns or quiet beach strolls. I waited behind the reception desk for the call.

It rang late, several minutes after the appointed time, but at least it rang and it was him:

'Strange choice of courier, Angelo. I wasn't sure what she was until she mentioned your name. Couldn't you have just posted it? She seemed confused, kept saying 'make sure he writes me in it' I just said yeah, yeah, okay I'll do that. I'm guessing you didn't tell her who I was?'

'No, I didn't. I thought that might put her off from the mission if she thought it was some sort of police work. I said you were a literary agent. I told her explicitly not to ask questions. Anyway, you took your time. So, what do you make of it?'

Interesting. I thought it was a joke at first, a funny face shot and I expected an accompanying pun attached, until I read your letter. I was

152

intrigued and took it in to the station, wired it along with the name and ran an international file check. It seems Hector Thanos is an entrepreneur and property developer. He's been trying for an application to develop a holiday complex for the rich in one of the resorts there, but been knocked back over the years.'

'That sounds about right. He's been trying to buy out the hoteliers here to change the profile of the resort, as he puts it. A more sophisticated tourist, he says he wants. He's a fanatic and he's as much as admitted it. There's something not quite right with him. I just can't put a finger on what it is, but I believe he's something to do with all the weird stuff that's been happening over here.'

'I heard about that. I take it you're okay yourself. Anyway, there's no photo of him on file so far. And you say this is a photo of Hector Thanos, right? Odd angle you took, I must say.'

'I didn't take it. He doesn't like being photographed. He accidentally took one of himself. He hadn't seen an Ektra camera before and was fiddling with it while trying to take one of me with his cheetah, but didn't realise it.'

'Cheetah? He owns a big cat? Sounds like a real eccentric.'

'That's right. I'll tell you about that later. Any more feedback on Thanos? Is he on any of your files?'

'Hector Thanos isn't on any wanted list, if that's what you're digging at. But this face isn't him. This photo you sent is a perfect match, a photo-fit for someone else.'

'Who?'

'I'm afraid I can't disclose that information, Angelo. This is a case for Interpol and any leaked information may hamper their co-operations. It's all in hand and this Hector Thanos persona is about to be intercepted. We have classified information that he's about to flee to a country out of our extradition treaties. Your photo confirmed the real identity of someone on their list. Nice work, Angelo, it seems your hunch about Thanos was right.'

'So what do I do now?'

'Nothing. You don't go doing anything stupid now. You haven't done anything stupid, have you?'

'Certainly not,' I lied. I couldn't possibly tell Dreyfus the truth at this point; it was far too late for that.

'If it's any consolation, Angelo, we already have a man out there cooperating with us.'

'Who?'

'His name is Castellanos.'

24.

Dreyfus would tell me nothing of the operation. Interpol knew that Thanos – whoever he really was – was absconding. He wouldn't tell me when or to where, only that I was raving like a madman. I was. The call became heated. Dreyfus confirmed it was the same Police Chief Elias Castellanos who was their co-operator in Corfu. I told Dreyfus about Castellanos being suspiciously there at the political rally explosion and barring my way when I wanted to follow what I thought was a suspect. I didn't say I suspected it was Thanos at that point. I told him about people unexpectedly dying, what the locals said about Castellanos being corrupt. I told him how Castellanos was desperate to get hold of the photo of Thanos, even searching my hotel room and harassing other guests. Dreyfus dismissed it as regular police work. He found it hard to understand why Thanos himself didn't ask for the roll of film with his self-photo. I told him what I thought, that Thanos must have not wanted to raise suspicion or draw attention to his self by demanding it, but I stuttered in my explanation. I was beginning to doubt myself and I'm sure that doubt carried over to Dreyfus. I really wanted to tell him about the beating I took at Castellanos' hand, but it was all too complicated, I'd have to admit to the assault charge and spending time in jail and admit to breaking into Thanos' mansion. He'd hang up at that. Dreyfus wouldn't cooperate at that and I had no evidence to prove anything from that other than what I'd seen. What I'd taken from Thanos' kitchen no longer existed and I'd taken it illegally anyway.

Dreyfus had only one more thing to say:

'Everything is in hand, Angelo. Interpol agents have all the details of his flight, departure date and destination. They've informed Greek agents who will be there to arrest him, question him and establish who he really is. They have your photo, thanks for that, it'll be most useful identifying him at his departure point, now leave it. Enjoy your holiday.'

'You don't understand!' I replied. 'Castellanos is in on this on Thanos' side. This departure date and flight times, I've no doubt are true, but don't you see this is just a decoy? Thanos won't be on that flight, he'll be long gone before you realise. He'll be getting off the island on another day at another point and going to an entirely different destination. Castellanos is nothing more than a Machiavellian rogue and Thanos is his puppet-master. It's a ruse and he's played you!'

'Damn it, Angelo, there is nothing on Castellanos. He's been vetted and he's above board. I'm sorry, Angelo, there's nothing else we can do. I can pass on what you've just said, but to be fair I think this is your writing mind getting ahead of you.'

'He made my shorts catch fire!' I blurted it out in exasperation.

He hung up.

'Not good news, Mr. Fox?' said Christos.

'No, Christos...not good.' I replaced the receiver feeling like a freshly gutted fish. 'It's best you take me to pick up my things from your house and take me to the airport, if you don't mind. I'll pay you for your help of course, Christos. It's over. I'll wait at the airport until the next flight either direct or nearest country transferring or a cancellation ticket. It's over. Castellanos has won.'

I didn't bother trying to hide. I explained Dreyfus' side of the conversation to Christos as I got in the Land Rover, not caring if Castellanos saw me or not. I imagined his smug, grinning face mocking me as Christos turned out of the Aeres' drive and headed out to Corfu International Airport. I wanted to say goodbye to Madge and Mabel, but they thought I had already left and were out somewhere in the resort enjoying the sea or sangria and I was in no mood to explain the situation or my sadness. That, I could do later. I vowed to phone the Aeres when I arrived back in the UK and make my apologies and meet again upon their own return.

I collected my suitcase from Christos' home and we continued the journey in silence.

I was missing something. Now that my mind was clear and all I had to think about was getting home, I realised a missed detail I'd almost forgotten about in all the confusion and drama of those last few days: A shifty looking little man in red and black check socks under sandals that drove a three-wheeled, little two-stroke flatbed wagon.

'Christos?' I asked. 'What do you know about the man who delivers the produce to the Aeres?'

'Balakros?'

'If that's his name. Yes. How well do you know him...this Balakros?'

'Balakros has supplied our hotel for many years,' said Christos.

'Yes, I imagine he has,' I said. 'But how well do you really know him? How much do you know about him? Do you know his family? His parents...brothers or sisters? What do you know about him?'

'A strange question, Mr. Fox. Why do you ask such a thing?'

'Just a thought, Christos. So, you know him very well, then...his family and everything? He's a trustworthy friend...like a brother to you, or a son to Elena? He's like that, I suppose?'

'Well...not really, Mr. Fox. I don't know about Balakros family. He is a trustworthy provider to all the hotels in Gouvia. He has done this for years and people like him, although he is very quiet and makes little conversation. He is not what you call...call...'

'Sociable?'

'Yes, that's what I mean,' said Christos. 'You don't see him in the taverns having a drink and playing cards like the rest of Gouvia folk. For what I know, he came from the mainland and has no family here in Gouvia. I'm still not sure what you are asking, Mr. Fox. It sounds like you are doubtful about Balakros, like you mistrust him somehow.'

'I don't.' I said. 'Perhaps I should have mentioned it before, Christos, but in all the confusion of past days, what with Castellanos harassing and arresting me and all, I'd quite forgotten about him. No, he isn't to be trusted and once I'm gone you should keep a keen eye on him. There's something not quite right about him, but it's too late to do anything now.'

'Please, explain what you mean, Mr. Fox?'

So, I told Christos what I'd seen and what I thought. I confessed how I'd followed him into one of the other hotels in Gouvia, pretending to be lost and making casual conversation about the hot weather. Then I told Christos how Balakros had dropped the dishes when I said the sun roars like a lion.

'But why would that disturb him?' said Christos.

'Because the words 'lion' and 'sun' disturbed him. He's been inside Liontari Ilion. I accidently found him out on the road that passes the mansion and saw him turn in there. He's been inside Hector Thanos' mansion.'

'Oh...that is strange. I didn't know Balakros delivered so far. Still, it is not unusual. Someone must supply goods to the place.'

'Only he wasn't delivering anything,' I said. 'His truck was empty. I was instantly suspicious, so I hid and waited for him. '

'Are you sure about this, Mr. Fox? That is very strange. Why would he visit there? So, what was he collecting? What did he have when he came out?'

'I'm quite sure it was him. I recognised the number plate on his vehicle. And he never came out. And I waited four hours.'

'Four hours?' said Christos. 'You waited four hours for him to come out?'

'Yes. Four hours. I timed it by my watch.'

Christos became silent for several minutes. He then turned sharply into the forecourt of a tavern and headed in the other direction.

'What are you doing, Christos?' I said.

'I want to talk to Balakros.'

'Right now? Can't it wait? Shouldn't you drop me off at the airport first?'

'Do you have a flight to catch?'

'Well, I'm not sure. I haven't booked it, but I explained this to you. I'll catch the next available one. I shouldn't hang around in Corfu any longer.'

'Then there is no problem,' said Christos. 'And I want you to be there when I speak to Balakros. You shall see why. And you can blame me if Castellanos sees you.'

25.

Christos drove all the way back to Gouvia. He turned down the narrow lane that led to the boat hire wharf, and parked up on the gravel beach. The distant sound of music and laughter drifted across a bay the colour of blue phthalo in the light of a half moon rising, silhouetting a little office shed on a wharf leading out to a collection of rowing boats, speedboats and pedalos that bobbed in the surf. A shanty house a few metres up the beach, partly obscured by pines glowed with an orange light from its one window. Out front was the little flatbed truck.

'This is where Balakros lives,' Christos said. 'He does some work for the wharf master between deliveries, when it is the busy season. It looks like he is in. Come, Mr. Fox.'

'He does some work for the wharf master?' I mumbled it. 'Filling petrol tanks might explain something.'

'Explain something?' said Christos. 'What does it explain?'

'It's what Philo was trying to tell me about sodium. The explosion on the boat here not long since. I believe it may have been caused by sodium in the petrol tank, but I can never prove that now.'

'Your pants by the pool? Philo said that was sodium.'

'Philo suggested that's what most likely caused it. I also believe it's one of the substances I found in Liontari Ilion. Castellanos missed it when he searched me, but it's gone now anyway.'

I followed Christos to the door and stood a few paces back while he knocked. A light went out and a shadow appeared at the window curtains. A minute later after some more knocks the light went back on. The door opened a few inches.

'Christos? What do you want?' The man sounded nervous.

'I wish to talk to you about our next order for the Aeres,'

said Christos.

'It is late, I will see you tomorrow.' He started to shut the door.

Christos put his foot in the way. 'No, Balakros. You will talk to me now.'

Balakros looked at the foot. He opened the door with a smile, a smile you have when someone sticks a foot in your door. When he saw me the smile dropped like a hot biscuit from a child's fist. 'What does *he* want?'

'I am driving Mr. Fox on his way to the airport. I'll only take a few moments of your time.'

Balakros pointed at me. 'He does not come in.'

'Why, Balakros?' said Christos. 'Mr. Fox is my friend and is leaving the island today. Please, this is not good for the island image to be unsociable to our visitors. Allow us in.'

Balakros stood back and we entered. We were offered neither seats nor drinks. Balakros remained standing. I could tell he wanted us to leave sooner than later. I wandered around the meagre-looking but tidy room, self-contained with a kitchen sink, sideboards, cupboards, a settee and lounge chair. There was an adjoining bedroom with no door and another half-opened door to a bathroom. Balakros' eyes followed me.

Christos got straight to the point: 'What were you doing in the Thanos place?'

Balakros glanced between us. He had the stare of a deer caught in headlights. 'Thanos?' he said. 'Who is Thanos?'

Christos glanced at me then back at Balakros. 'You lie. You know who I mean. Hector Thanos. Is he the man who tried to buy us out? The man who wanted to take the Aeres away from Mama, Philo and me? I think he sent those men to make us an offer and you know something about it. Do not deny this, Balakros. Why have you been to see Thanos?'

'No, I have nothing to do with him.'

Christos slammed a fist down on the table making Balakros

jerk and the crockery in the cupboards rattle. 'So you know who I mean?' he said. 'First you say you don't know Thanos, then you say you have nothing to do with him. You are a liar. Tell him, Mr. Fox.'

'I saw you,' I said. 'I saw you go into the mansion Liontari Ilion. I followed your truck. You didn't come out even after four hours. What were you doing there?'

'There is a mistake,' said Balakros. 'It was not me. It must be someone else. There are many trucks like mine in Corfu.'

'No, Balakros. I took a photo of your truck outside the Aeres. I remembered your registration plate. It was your registration that visited Hector Thanos. The same registration on the truck that stands outside. And I recognised a man of your stature, black hair, balding. There is no mistake. It was you.'

Balakros dithered like someone about to wet their pants. He stared at the floor. 'I have nothing to say. You are trying to bully me. Please leave now or I will call Castellanos.'

'Castellanos?' said Christos. 'Why Castellanos? Why not just call the police?'

'That is what I mean. I mean I will call the police.'

'No, you meant to say Castellanos. You are hiding something, Balakros. Hiding the truth and you will tell me now. Castellanos and Thanos are together in something. Mr. Fox has found something out and you also know what this is. Please tell me now Balakros, or this will go very badly for you.'

Balakros still wouldn't speak. I walked along by the sideboard cupboards and flung one open and Balakros squealed like a girl. 'Leave that and get out now, or things will go even more badly for you!'

'What are you afraid of, Balakros?' I said. 'Perhaps you are hiding more than just the truth?'

I flung two more cupboards open. Nothing. Balakros leapt for me and Christos held him back by the collar and shoved him into a chair. I checked the lower cabinets, same again. I wasn't sure exactly what I expected to find, just a hunch. I rifled the bathroom cabinet, then under the bed. There were two chunky A4 size manila envelopes between the mattress and frame.

I rifled the wardrobe next. I pulled clothes off hangers, throwing them onto the bed. A jacket slipped off its hanger onto the floor and out they came. Out onto the floor from one of the pockets spilled plastic phials. Little plastic phials, same as the ones I found in Thanos' kitchen. Same as the one that leaked and blew up my shorts. I sniffed one. No smell, but that didn't matter, I'd seen enough. I grabbed a handful, along with the envelopes and came back into the room, throwing them all on the table.

'Very clumsy, Balakros,' I said. 'Didn't Thanos instruct you to get rid of these, or maybe you thought you didn't need to as Castellanos would protect you? Or more likely, I suspect you had every intention of using them again upon Thanos' instruction. Isn't that why you went to see him with an empty truck? No need to deliver anything that day, just some instruction. A little reward and something to collect, then come back out under the cover of darkness, is that it? And what about these?'

I tore an envelope open, spilling the contents onto the table. A lot of Drachma in used notes. Mixed denominations, but some amount of cash to be vacant from a bank account. I tore the other one open. Another fat wad. 'Business doing well then, Balakros?'

'Not your business!' Balakros snarled.

Christos lost it at that. He yanked Balakros up by the collar and shoved him bent face down at the table, twisting his left arm up behind his back.

'Our business!' Christos yelled. 'You are a liar! Maybe you are friends with Castellanos also, are you? To think that we trusted you all this time and you were working against us. You will talk now or I will break your lying fucking arm and neck. I have my friend in jail, our hotel business is about to disappear, Mama is in despair and you know something about it.'

'Steady on, Christos,' I said. 'We only want one thing from him and I think he knows the answer. Tell me, Balakros, when is Thanos leaving the island...and where from? You must know this. You have these phials, the same type I found in Hector Thanos' kitchen. You used them to go about his dreadful business for him. You got these from him to distribute poisons and disease, and I believe volatile chemicals around Gouvia. I know Thanos is leaving the island soon, so you must know that also. Is he taking his accomplice with him? Taking you? So, when is he leaving Corfu?'

'You are both fools,' said Balakros. 'You don't know who you are dealing with. You are both dead men now.'

'You are the fool, Balakros,' I said. 'Can't you see how he's used you? You will go to prison for a very long time for your part, and I'm certain now that you are very much a part of Thanos' scheme to get the hoteliers to sell up. You would lose your delivery business if that happened. But now you will lose your freedom, probably for the rest of your life by taking the rap for Thanos. So Thanos must have promised you a very handsome sum in compensation for the loss of your business, something considerably more than this cash. I would call this a paltry sum for what Thanos has asked of you. How much was it, Balakros? How much more blood money has he crossed your palm with? Or perhaps you are going with him? Is this what he has told you? Maybe you've emptied your bank account to take with you. Thanos is an unscrupulous man, he may have promised you this, but I doubt he'll take you with him. Oh no, far too much baggage. Better to leave you here to take the blame, even though he is no doubt the perpetrator of the mayhem in Gouvia. So, it is better that you talk to us now.'

Balakros squeaked like a mouse. 'I have nothing to say.'

Christos wrenched the arm up harder and Balakros howled in agony. Christos palmed the back of his head hard, slamming it face first onto the table with a hideous bang. It stopped the howling. I doubted anyone was near enough that night to have heard, but no doubt Christos was taking no chances.

Balakros raised his head. Blood droplets sprinkled the table top. 'Dead men,' he groaned.

Christos' mood scared me. But we were in it too deep now. Balakros was no doubt in league with Castellanos and that scared me more. It was enough knowing that Castellanos knew I was still on the island. But if he happened to wander by that night we really would be 'dead men.' Thanos was on Interpol's list of internationally wanted criminals and Castellanos would probably be our executioner at his order if he knew what we were doing. But we had to continue. Part of me wished Christos had dropped me off at the airport first, but it was way too late. I was complicit. Whatever Thanos was wanted for, Castellanos was helping him to escape. I knew it, Christos knew it and Balakros knew how and when.

'You will tell us what you know, Balakros,' said Christos.

'Dead men,' said Balakros. 'You are both dead when he finds out. When I tell Castellanos about this, you are dead men.'

'So you admit Castellanos is in on this?' I said. 'Now tell us when Thanos intends leaving; then we will leave you at peace.' I hadn't really thought it through, but there was no doubt now that we could hardly leave Balakros in peace. I was hoping Christos would come up with something, something short of beating the man to death.

'He will talk,' said Christos. 'Get me some cloth.'

I looked around and snatched a tea towel from a hook by the sink.

'When he opens his mouth, shove it in,' said Christos. Then

he wrenched the arm even further. Balakros barely had time to yell. In went the tea towel, as much as I could stuff.

Still holding two hands on his locked arm, Christos kneed him into the base of the spine, not hard, but enough. Balakros' eyes popped, tears came and mixed with blood droplets from his nose. 'Pull the towel out, Mr. Fox.'

I did as instructed. Balakros panted and wheezed like a man on his death bed.

'Now tell us when Thanos is leaving,' said Christos.

'Dead...men...'

'Again, Mr. Fox.'

Once again, a little harder this time, Christos rammed his knee into Balakros' spine. I shoved the towel back in before anything came out. Christos kneed him three more times. 'See if he speaks now, Mr. Fox.'

I pulled the towel out. Balakros seemed incapable of speech.

'I can go on all night like this Balakros,' said Christos. 'It matters not to me. You have a choice. Tell us what you know about Thanos and I stop and I let you live. If you tell us I will hide you away where Castellanos can't reach you. If you don't I keep punishing you like this until you die. Then I take you out onto the sea and drop you in with an anchor.'

I held the towel to Balakros' face. 'He means it,' I said. 'It's either you speak now, we stop and give you protection, or Christos' choice. I don't think Christos wants to stop. I think he's just warming up. So when is Thanos leaving?'

Balakros had a wild, terrified look in his eyes. 'S, s, Sunday,' he whimpered.

'Sunday?' I said. 'Which Sunday?'

'Tom...next Sunday...'

'Next Sunday? You didn't mean that. You were going to say tomorrow, weren't you?'

No answer.

Christos kneed Balakros once again and Balakros erupted in

agony. I shoved the towel in. I was going to pull it out, but Christos made me leave it in longer. He was turning colour.

'I think he's going to pass out,' I said.

'Pull it out, Mr. Fox. This is his last call. He tells us now or I finish him.'

I pulled the towel out.

Balakros gasped and wheezed.

'Tomorrow...yes...tomorrow...Thanos leaves.'

'What time and where?' I said.

'Twelve. Twelve noon. From Heliakos. There is a cove. He is being collected and leaving by yacht precisely at twelve. They will not wait longer. The people have told him once only, his one chance to flee.'

'Where to?'

'I don't know this,' said Balakros. 'Please, I don't know this. He would not tell me. I am to go with him. I am to meet them in the morning.'

'Them? Who would that be?'

'Big men. Big men with big faces and big hands. Everything big. Big men in the crime world. Mafiosos. This is what I mean when I say you don't know what you are dealing with. When I say you are dead men. I am to be at Liontari Ilion at eleven latest. I am to go with Thanos. If I am not there Thanos will go, he will not wait, but they will hunt me down and kill me for what I know and they will kill you if they find out you have stopped me. Thanos is taking me with him for security.'

'Mafiosos?' I said. 'Mafia. Oh dear, Balakros, don't you see? Thanos wants you to go with him for security alright. Thanos wants you to go so you won't talk. He and these mafiosos will make sure of that. Wherever he's going, somewhere on the trip they'll drop you in the middle of the ocean. You've done his dirty work and he can't risk you being left behind to squeal. But we can't let you go just like that. No, you have to stay here until all this is sorted out. You see, international agents are about to get Thanos, so your best bet is to remain with us and tell them everything you know. Maybe they'll go easy on you if you spill the beans on Thanos and Castellanos. Am I right? Castellanos is in on this departure too, isn't he, Balakros?'

'Yes...Castellanos. Castellanos is making sure Thanos meets his people.'

I looked at Christos. 'I think we've heard enough. What do we do with him now? We haven't got much time and I need to get this new information to Dreyfus as soon as possible before Thanos can escape. We can hardly let him go.' I was scared of the answer.

'What would Jimmy Finn do?' said Christos.

'Right now he'd tell you to stop listening to two old ladies.'

'We tie him up and hide him then.'

'Have you got rope?'

'In the back of the Rover. How do you think I rescue motorcycles you English run over the cliffs?'

We bound Balakros up, blindfolded and tea towel stuffed him, threw him in the back of the Rover, struggling and muffling protests. I stuffed the money and phials into a pillowcase and rode in the back with him to Christos' homestead.

Christos hid the pillowcase of money and phials under a stone and rubble pile at the gable end of the house. We removed Balakros' blindfold and gag and padlocked him in the cellar with a bowl of water he'd have to drink from like a dog with a promise to be only a few hours. It was the middle of the night and a few hours was all we had. We shut him in. Shutting the cellar door we could barely hear his shouts upstairs in the kitchen. Outside, he was inaudible. It didn't matter anyway; he could shout his head off.

The nearest house was a mile away.

We arrived back at the Aeres in the middle of the night. I

rang and knew Dreyfus wouldn't appreciate being woken, but I thought he'd soon be wide-eyed and bushy-tailed when I passed on this new information.

He didn't answer. He didn't answer all night long. The night wore on, Elena and Philo awoke to start the day's preparations, totally flummoxed to see me and equally puzzled as to where Christos had disappeared to.

'No time to explain, Mama,' said Christos. 'Mr. Fox has important information, please let him keep calling. Trust me, the Aeres will be saved if Mr. Fox gets through.'

'Oh, stop with the Mr. Fox, please, Christos,' I said. 'Call me Angelo. Better still, call me Jimmy Finn again, for heaven's sake, I might as well be him.'

I kept phoning to no avail. Time was evaporating like poolside puddles in the heat of a Corfu summer. 'I don't know what we do now, Christos. I do believe Dreyfus is ignoring the call, possibly for security reasons, probably more like I must have sounded like some deranged person last time we spoke.'

'You could keep trying,' said Christos. 'But there is not much time left, maybe three hours. Thanos will be leaving for Heliakos soon. Once he is there, we can do nothing.'

I tried a few more times. We had to do something on our own. I didn't know what, but somehow we had to delay Thanos from reaching his departure point. We needed help. We needed help from someone who had no run-ins with Castellanos, preferably someone who didn't even know of his name. Someone who liked a challenge; someone who had a sense of adventure and didn't give a flying fuck about safety.

Kevin the Club 18-30 beer can chucker.

26.

'You want me to do...whaaat?'

Kevin sat in a leather arm chair, his feet up on a coffee table in the lobby of the hotel formerly called the Odyssey. He was alone, ticking off something on a clipboard. A cockroach popped out from the chair beneath him. I imagined it was equally as surprised as Kevin. It popped back under, dodging Kevin's quick as lightning foot. 'Little bastards,' he said. 'Another one missed.'

'Throw a surprise birthday party,' I said.

Kevin stared at me like I was another cockroach, appearing out of nowhere and uninvited.

'It's quite simple,' I said. 'This friend of mine has arrived on the island. I'd quite forgotten he was coming and it's his birthday today. I'd forgotten that as well and I'd promised him I'd arrange and celebrate with him upon his arrival. He sent me a telegram that he was coming and hoped I hadn't forgotten my promise. Well I had, until this morning when I got his message. It's a milestone, you see. He's forty today. And I haven't organised anything.'

Kevin was silent. His magnified eyes stared at me through thick as ice cubes, gold rimmed lenses like he had X-ray specs on. Maybe it was the dress. I'd gone out to buy a Greek baseball cap and an 'I love Gouvia' tee-shirt, with a heart symbol where the word love should be and some extra large round-rimmed sunglasses. I looked ridiculous. In Gouvia I fitted in. I also felt ridiculous. But I fitted in.

I'd disguised myself so my birthday friend wouldn't recognise me at first. That was the bullshit I gave Kevin. Kevin liked that. I wanted a few people who liked a party to help us celebrate. Kevin liked that too. So if a few of the Club 18-30 would like to come along and make a party of it, they're welcome.

Kevin thought about it. 'I'm not sure about this. Forty, eh? We're supposed to be a club for eighteen to thirty year olds.'

'Some of your guests look sixty.'

'That's alcohol for you.'

'I'll pay for all the drinks.'

Kevin liked that most of all.

'Well...it is a Sunday,' said Kevin. 'I usually let the guys rest on Sundays. But we do have a weekly mystery tour, which is a drive out to somewhere they haven't been previously and have a beach party. And they do like surprises. That's what Club 18-30 is all about. Fun and surprises. I suppose I could see if any of them are up for it. I'll go rouse a few, most are still sleeping it off.'

It was going to be a surprise, alright. Fun? To be announced.

'You look ridiculous,' said Madge.

'I feel ridiculous,' I said.

'And what are you doing back in Corfu?'

'I never left.'

'I might have guessed. You're up to something, I can tell.'

'Nothing gets past you, does it?'

'Well, it's not as if the get-up isn't a dead giveaway,' said Madge. 'A respectable middle-aged man dressing like an unruly teenage delinquent? What are you doing exactly?'

'I can't say,' I said. 'Thanks for the compliment, by the way.'

'What compliment?'

'Middle-aged. I'm in my fifties.'

'That makes you even more ridiculous. Grow up, for heaven's sake and tell us what gives.'

'It's complicated.'

'I'm not bailing you out this time.'

'You didn't first time. That was Thanos, remember?'

'It still cost me. You owe us an explanation, at least.'

'An explanation,' Mabel repeated.

I had no time for explanations. And standing around in the Aeres' reception area looking ridiculous in front of puzzled guests wasn't helping. I had to go. Christos had pulled up outside in the Rover and was beeping the horn.

'We can help,' said Mabel.

'Sorry,' I said. 'I can't let you. All will come clear eventually...hopefully.'

Outside, two more Jeep convertibles had pulled up at the end of the drive, beeping horns, laughing youngsters and disco music blaring out from a ghetto-blaster.

'Gotta go,' I said and ran out, hopping in next to Christos who churned gravel out to the road.

'Angelo Fox, get back here this instant!' was the last cry from Madge as we headed out. I heard a response from Mabel. It was a cried repeat of Madge's call, fast fading away into the ghetto-blast of 'Oops Upside You're Head' as we zoomed away.

Christos had pointed out the one and only thing in our plan that was in our favour. There was only one narrow road in or out of the port of Heliakos. I could see why Thanos wanted it so remote. I could see why any gangsters would want it so remote. Its solitude sounded the ideal retreat for smugglers, or escaping international criminals. If we could delay Thanos just long enough to miss his pick-up, it would be job done. He'd still be on the island by the time Interpol got their act together and realised he wasn't catching any plane. Christos pointed out that Thanos might already be at the port. He also pointed out that this was the dumbest, most dangerous and scatter-brained idea he'd ever heard of. He actually said that and I can't imagine where he picked up that expression from.

'But why do we need all these rowdy kids?' said Christos.

'It's cover, Christos,' I said. 'It bides us some time. If there were just the two of us, Thanos or Castellanos would quickly recognise me. Their attention will be diverted in a crowd and they'll concentrate on shifting the Rover. I'll simply blend in as a party-goer.'

Christos glanced at me with a wry smile. 'A party-goer? You look like an old man in a naughty teenager's outfit.'

'Charming. You'd best hope Thanos doesn't notice.'

Christos pointed out that I hadn't told the truth to Kevin.

I asked him what else he thought about it.

He loved it.

Christos headed the convoy. We pulled into a lay-by past an ideal narrow curve in the road, a gentle curve allowing a view of any vehicles approaching from behind. We were about two miles outside of the port. We allowed the two Club Jeeps to pass and park in the lay-by a few metres further down. Christos backed up into the narrowest section of the bend, blocking the road. Beer cans were opened, the music turned up and half a dozen girls and boys that weren't still hung over jumped out of the Jeeps drinking and laughing and waiting for the 'big surprise' to be sprung. Surprise it would be alright. Not the one they were expecting.

'This is crazy,' said Kevin. 'Can't you just wait for your friend in port?'

'Trust me,' I said. 'He'll totally get this. It's his sense of humour and the least expected thing will really amuse him. He once did something like it to me. Just keep him occupied for a while, while I pretend to be someone else, like one of you guys.'

'Apart from the tee-shirt, cap and stupid sunglasses, you don't look like one of us.'

'I'll keep out of the way then. I'll wander off, pretending to take a leak or even taking a leak. I take a lot of leaks at my age.

I'll have my back turned until the moment of surprise. That will be when he starts getting really impatient and annoyed and then I'll spring out. He'll love it.'

'I hope so,' said Kevin. 'I mean you won't let it get to the stage where he gets violent, will you?'

I wished he hadn't said that. 'No, trust me, he'll love it.' I couldn't guarantee what Thanos would or would not do, if he turned up at all.

I'd explained it to Kevin. I wasn't sure exactly what time my 'friend' was due to arrive, but what we were to do is leave the Land Rover parked in the middle of the road, pretending to have broken down and effectively blocking the way. Then if any ordinary folk came in or out of the port, Christos would simply move the Rover to the lay-by and let them pass, then back it up to the narrow space again. When my 'friend' arrived, the breakdown story remained. We'd hold him there – or them if Castellanos was accompanying him – until the twelve noon deadline passed and it was too late for Thanos to make his connection. It wouldn't be easy, especially if we had to hold them for any lengthy period. It wouldn't take Thanos or Castellanos that long to recognise me, ridiculous hat and shirt or not, or for Kevin to get suspicious, or panicky if Castellanos started making threats. But I knew Christos would keep the act going as long as possible. The worst case scenario would be to find Castellanos making his way up from the port in an empty car, having delivered Thanos' escape.

Explaining the truth to Kevin and party that they could all be arrested hadn't been factored in. Kevin and party would eventually realise that my friend didn't exist and they'd been used. But with a man tied up and bundled away, an innocent man in prison and a good friend with his mother's hotel business at risk, we felt there was no other choice.

There was nothing else to do but wait. We let three vehicles through to the port and one out who'd driven in half an hour previously, a three-wheeled, flatbed, two-stroke truck delivering vegetables, the driver of which asked how we managed to break down again in exactly the same spot.

The next vehicle puzzled me. The whole time I'd spent on the island I didn't remember seeing a single taxi outside of the main Corfu Town itself. Locals didn't use them. Kids and holidaymakers either hired cars and bikes or used the local buses, which were frequent, cheap and time-reliable.

I alerted Christos and raised the Rover's bonnet, concealing myself from view. Christos hopped into the driver's seat pretending to try and start it, turning the key on and off again, while I watched, glancing around the bonnet in my big stupid sunglasses as the taxi pulled up behind.

The taxi driver beeped his horn repeatedly. That was suspicious. Corfu people don't do urgency, but this guy seemed frantic, pounding his fist on the horn. Christos hopped out of the seat with a spanner, a screwdriver and crowbar and shrugged his shoulders at the taxi driver and came round to the front. I was trying desperately to get a look at the taxi passenger.

'I think this is him,' I said to Christos. I wasn't absolutely sure, but the figure looked like Thanos. He was close, disturbingly close, like I could sense his presence and sense my own stark visibility in my silly disguise.

We didn't have to wait long. Both driver and passenger got out. I nudged Christos. He quickly got to work, unclipping the Rover's distributor cap and spinning it a half turn. He went round and confronted the two. It was Thanos alright. Christos explained to him he'd soon have the Rover shifted. Then he climbed underneath it and did 'the business.' He later explained how he jammed the crowbar between the front wheel and damper.

Thanos looked at his watch. 'What is the problem? I have business to attend to. How long?'

'Two minutes,' said Christos. 'Just a little starting problem, I think. I apologise.'

'I'll have a look, if you don't mind,' said Thanos.

I took the cue, turned away and wandered off to the Jeeps, but still near enough to hear. I pulled my cap over, part shielding my face and leaned on one of the vehicles, pretending to act cool and watched. I spoke quietly to the others, making polite chat. They got it, believing my low voice and fraternizing were part of the act leading to the 'big surprise.' It was also a ruse to pull one more planned trick while Thanos was preoccupied.

Thanos came round to the front of the Rover, Christos climbed out from underneath and hopped in the driver's seat and turned the ignition. The engine spluttered, backfired and died.

'I can see the problem,' said Thanos. 'Your timing is out. You have some tools, hand me a screwdriver.'

Christos jumped out and came round to the front. 'You can't do it like that. If it's the timing you need point feeler gauges. I don't carry them.'

'No, no, there is another way if you let me try,' said Thanos. 'Your distributor appears to be loose on its mount. If I spin it a little, tighten it, then you try to start it. If it's backfiring worse, then you spin it a little in the other direction, then try again. It's a little trial and error to get it right, but you keep trying it see, until it's somewhere near correct firing. It's not perfect, but it will get it running well enough to move it and get you home, or to a garage.'

'It's also bad for the engine,' said Christos.

'You also don't have much choice out here without your feeler gauges. You have to get home and I have business.'

Christos played along. Thanos spun the distributor, Christos got back in the Rover and tried the key again. Thanos was lucky and the engine fired. Christos immediately turned the ignition off. Thanos tried again. This time it backfired and died on its own. Christos acted out the charade a few more times, allowing the car to run backfiring, or killing the engine if it fired up normally. Thanos scratched his head.

'Is this the guy?' one of the kids asked me.

'Yes, it's him,' I said. 'But be patient, this will be fun, trust me. Don't do anything yet, just have another beer in the meantime. He'll love it when he finds out it's me.'

He certainly would not, I thought.

Another car arrived. A police car. It was going fast for a narrow lane with bends and screeched to a halt behind the taxi. Castellanos immediately jumped out. He came round to Thanos fiddling under the bonnet.

'What is this?' Castellanos asked.

'A little engine trouble,' said Thanos. 'Something else must be wrong. I thought it was an ignition problem, but no. I've tried the distributor in every position, but still the engine dies.'

Thanos straightened up and slammed the bonnet down. 'So, where is he?' he asked Castellanos.

'I have looked everywhere,' said Castellanos. 'Not at the house or the boatyard. He has run off.'

'It doesn't matter,' said Thanos. 'Deal with him after...if you're capable of that even.'

'He has taken things with him. The payments, evidence...'

'Shut up, you fool! We have no time for him now. Just deal with him when you find him.'

They didn't have to name him. I knew who they were talking about.

'Get this thing out of the way now!' Thanos yelled. He pointed to the taxi driver and Castellanos. 'You and you help. We'll push it.'

The three of them gathered at the rear of the Rover, pushing while Christos manned the steering wheel. It didn't budge.

Thanos leapt round to the driver's seat. 'Get out, idiot! I know when someone is pissing me about.'

'The handbrake is off,' said Christos. 'It's four-wheel drive, very heavy.'

'Take it out of gear then!'

Christos showed him that the gear stick was in neutral and the handbrake off.

'Get out anyway, idiot. I'll do it. Push it when I say.'

Christos got out and Thanos jumped in the driver's seat. Three pushed from behind. The Rover was locked in place, immovable. Crow-barred, you could say.

'When are we doing it?' Kevin asked. 'That's a copper. He's not going to like it if we don't get out of the way.'

'Not long now,' I said. I looked at my watch. Thanos would still make his connection if we let him pass then.

'I think this has gone on long enough,' said Kevin. He signalled one of the kids and 'Happy Birthday' blared out of the ghetto-blaster.

Thanos was quickly losing his cool, I could tell. He jumped out of the Rover and marched down to the Jeeps. I turned my back and did what I thought was happy birthday dancing to the amusement of the other kids.

'I've had enough of this,' said Thanos. 'One of you will drive me into port in one of your vehicles. Who is in charge here?'

Kevin put his hand up. 'That's me.' I glanced round and smiled at him innocently. Kevin looked at me with a puzzled frown.

'Get in,' said Thanos. He pointed to the lead Jeep.

Kevin still played along and hopped in the Jeep. Thanos followed. Kevin looked around, feeling at the dashboard and under his seat. 'Where's the key?' he said. 'Sorry, I seem to have misplaced it.'

'The other one,' said Thanos. 'Quickly, do not waste my

time.' He got in the other Jeep and Kevin followed.

The same thing happened. 'Alright, which joker has the keys?' asked Kevin.

There was silence. The kids looked at each other innocently. That's when my worst nightmare manifested. Thanos pulled a gun from his pants and pointed it into Kevin's temple. 'Enough playing games now. One of you will hand over the keys or I shoot him here and now. I am not fooling.'

'Jesus, Angelo,' said Kevin. 'You didn't tell me about this.'

27.

'Angelo?' Thanos spun round in his seat. Kevin tried to move, but Thanos spun back, grabbed him by the hair and pushed the gun to his temple again. It didn't take him long to filter me out from the others. 'Angelo Fox? What in god's name are you doing here?'

'Well, I suppose I could ask you the same question,' I said. 'Now if you don't mind, I'll ask you kindly to put the gun down.'

'Sorry, Mr. Fox, but I have some business in Heliakos and will get there at all costs. I will kill him if necessary.'

'And right here in front of the Chief of Police. I wonder...how is that possible without being arrested? Very strange, I think.'

'Perhaps you think too much, Mr. Fox. If I'm not away from this shower of reprobates in ten seconds, I blow this young man's brains all over the road. So, if you know something about these keys, you best say so right now.'

'For Christ's sake, man!' cried Kevin. 'Someone give him the keys!'

I reached into my pocket and held them up. Two sets of Jeep keys. My little extra ruse had backfired catastrophically.

'Throw them over, Mr. Fox,' said Thanos. He pushed the gun hard into Kevin's temple.

'Not so fast, Thanos,' I said. 'You let the lad go first. If you're taking any hostage, then it's going to be me. I'll drive you into port.'

Thanos thought about it. Not for long. He smiled. 'You are a clever man, Mr. Fox. But you underestimate me. If you try anything, don't think I won't shoot you as easily as this boy. As much as I respect you, I will dismiss you from this earth just as easily. Very well then, you drive.'

Thanos lifted his gun and Kevin got out. Thanos waved the kids away. They ran up towards Castellanos as if he was to help. Castellanos had watched the drama and had recognised me, I'm certain. But oddly, he didn't approach us.

Another vehicle was coming. Castellanos' car was on the bend and the new arrival was going way too fast for the road. It swung round the bend and screeched too late, a little Seat, thumping to a halt into the back of Castellanos' cop car. Out jumped two very familiar and apologetic ladies. Castellanos ran back and was soon raging, throwing his arms about and shouting at them.

Madge and Mabel soon spotted me. If I hadn't dressed up like an idiot they might not have noticed. They started running towards me. I waved them away. They saw the gun and stopped.

'Ignore them and get in the Jeep,' said Thanos.

I got in and started the Jeep, Thanos climbed in, pointing the gun at my head. I drove down the lane towards the port of Heliakos and god knows what else might be waiting for me.

A few minutes later Thanos ordered me to pull up in a lay-by a short distance from the port. He still held the gun at me. A Luger, I'd noticed, the significance of which tantalised, but eluded me and made me even more uncomfortable.

'Why didn't you just take the Jeep?' I said. 'You didn't need me.'

'Clever, Mr. Fox,' said Thanos. 'But as much as I respect you, I don't trust you. And why should I trust someone who breaks into my home? Although I think that was very clever, how you did it. But you made mistakes, a little amateurish, I think. But also, I think you may have tried something else today.'

'Such as?'

'Perhaps you might have booby-trapped the Jeep? I don't know. So, your suggestion to take you instead of the boy has played into my hand. You volunteering suggested to me that you might not have wanted the boy to be in any danger, if you had rigged something, so you took his place. Then perhaps, you had planned to jump from the Jeep at the right time? I don't know. But you see I did not intend any of this. I was going to leave quietly, but you had to get further involved, I don't know how or why, but it doesn't surprise me, a man of your intelligence. I assume Balakros is somehow involved in your being informed? How did you know? What have you done with him?'

I said nothing.

'It doesn't matter,' said Thanos. 'Balakros will be dealt with in due course. My people will see to that. You are a very intriguing man, Mr. Fox, but you made an amateur's mistake. I didn't need a hostage at all, I only wanted a driver. At first I simply wanted one of them to drive me into port, not hijack a vehicle. Now that has caused alarm and suspicion, which I wanted to avoid. But, your silly prank didn't work did it? Then I had to do something to get moving quickly. So I had to make the threat. If you hadn't taken the Jeep keys, all would have gone ahead without any problems or suspicion. And then you assumed I was going to take your boy as hostage and you volunteered to take his place. Very noble of you, but I had no intention of taking him, or anyone else along as a hostage. I just wanted the passage into port. Your assumption was good fortune for me, because I think you are still capable of doing something radically stupid. Amateurish, prone to mistakes, but I think I know you enough now to realise you might try. In the meantime, while you are here, Castellanos will play along, pretending that this is a hostage situation. He will fake some broadcast on his CB that police backup has been alerted and assure all your co-conspirators there that all is in hand and they should remain calm and where they are until the 'hostage' situation is resolved. That way no one does anything stupid, Castellanos gets the chance to, to, how should I say it...reason with them, and I get away.'

'You mean threaten them,' I said. 'I didn't think Castellanos was that intelligent. I even think my two friends back there could outwit him.'

'So those are your two lady friends you spoke of? A little old, don't you think?'

'The clue is in the word 'friends.' Are you going to shoot me now?'

'I should do.'

'So why have we stopped here? We're nearly at the port.'

'I don't want you to see any more.' Thanos looked at his watch. 'I would call it bad luck for you to see my departure. I don't want my people to see that my pickup has been anything other than smooth and uninterrupted. That would arouse suspicion on their part. And I don't trust you not to do anything stupid in port, although that would surely get you shot, but not by me. I'll walk it from here. I have just enough time to get my passage.'

'I think I've seen enough already,' I said.

'You have no clue, Mr. Fox. You see, I have multiple pickups on my passage, not just the boat, and all arranged by my people. No one will ever trace my voyage.'

Out to sea a helicopter hovered. Thanos looked up, alerted by the faint whir of its blades in the distance. 'It looks like one is nearby already to follow and connect, Mr. Fox. Where and when exactly, nobody knows. Just one of many connections at untraceable and random points. The good news, Mr. Fox is that I'm not going to shoot you. It would be a shame to do that. I've also told Castellanos to lay off you. He'll leave you alone, no more harassing or threatening. It's over now, you can go in peace. So, I will bid you farewell. It's been interesting to meet you.'

Thanos climbed out of the Jeep, holding the gun at me and backed up along the lane a way, then turned and jogged towards the port. I sat a while and thought about following. I'm not sure why, or even if it would help anyone to get a look at the yacht and its maritime number. It probably didn't display one anyway, and I believed that Thanos, or one of his people would shoot me on sight. So I sat there in quiet contemplation harbouring a deep sense of failure.

The Land Rover appeared not long after and pulled up alongside. 'I was worried about you,' said Christos.

'I see you got it running alright,' I said.

'Of course. I put a little scratch on the distributor and disguised it with my greasy hands so I knew where to reset it. Thanos never noticed. So here we are. Are you okay?'

'Yes, I'm fine. What's happening up the road?'

'Not much. Everyone's gone home except for your two friends.'

'In one Jeep?'

'They're Club 18-30,' said Christos. 'That's just like any other of their stupid games, seeing how many they can stuff in a Jeep, then driving off to the beach to get drunk. There were only six of them and Kevin. That's nothing for those guys. I saw them get ten in one day. After Castellanos left, they just wanted to get out of there. Nobody wanted to follow you and find a body at the side of the road. Kevin says leave the other Jeep at the Aeres, he'll pick it up later...if you're not dead. As for Madge and Mabel, they're waiting for you and praying you are alright.'

'Blast them,' I said. 'I just know this was no coincidence.

How they knew to follow us I can't imagine. I apologise for this whole debacle, Christos. It seems we've failed and he's got off the island.'

'Don't worry. It's been fun being a Jimmy Finn. We should go back and count our blessings.'

'Whatever they may be.' I started the Jeep.

28.

'Well, well, well, if it isn't Harold Lloyd himself,' said Madge. She was leaning off the bonnet of the convertible Seat as we pulled up. Her arms were folded like an angry wife confronting a drunken husband late home from the pub.

I got out of the Jeep. 'Harold Lloyd? Why Harold Lloyd?'

'Comedian and actor who took unnecessary risks with stupid stunts,' said Madge.

'I think he's more like Lloyd the comedian,' said Mabel. She was sat with her legs out of the passenger door, fanning herself.

'Well, at least I know who that is this time,' I said. 'So, what happened here?'

'Oh no,' said Madge. 'Angelo Fox, Jimmy Finn or whoever else you think you are, first you tell us what's happened, why you never left Corfu when you said you were leaving, why you took off so suddenly dressed like an adolescent-minded adult on this ridiculous and dangerous wild goose chase. You put yourself and lots of other people in danger. Those poor kids were shaking, some of them. They were petrified.' The folded arms unfolded and the hands found her hips. All that was missing was a rolling pin.

Christos jumped out of the Rover. 'Do not be angry with Mr. Fox. This was my idea too. I begged Mr. Fox to let me help.'

'Either way, you have some explaining to do,' said Madge. 'Why are you here?'

'I can't explain that just yet,' I said. 'But, I'm afraid it's all been a waste. That was Hector Thanos and he's gone. Whoever he is, he's escaped justice.'

'We know who it was,' said Madge. 'You don't have to tell us. Castellanos told us and he also said you were now a dead man, that Thanos would eliminate you for trying to stop him.

Stupid. Just stupid.'

'Stupid,' repeated Mabel.

'Well, you shouldn't have followed,' I said. 'Why did you? That was equally as stupid. I couldn't tell you because I knew you'd either follow or talk me out of it.'

'We were worried about you,' said Madge. 'You lied to us. You were acting out of character again. And we knew you were up to something, we knew you were going to do something stupid again, as if breaking into his home wasn't stupid enough.'

'How did you know where to follow?'

'Well, when we saw you jump in the Rover with Christos we asked Philo if he knew anything. He denied it at first, until we bribed him with a little cash. Apparently he overheard you two discussing it this morning after you kept trying to phone someone back in the UK'

'And what about Castellanos? Where is he?'

'He let the Club kids go first,' said Madge. 'But not until he'd told them all they'd seen nothing, it was not their business and if they wanted to get back to the UK safely they should keep quiet and say nothing to anyone, either here or back home. They were scared of him. We backed up and let Kevin and the kids out then Castellanos left soon after. He said he'd deal with us both later. I was tempted to ask him what he was doing there. It seemed too much of a coincidence, but like those Club kids, we were scared of him too. After the kids left he kept saying what he was going to do with you when you came back, but then this helicopter flew by and hovered over us for a minute. He seemed to get spooked by it and left rather hurriedly.'

'It was no coincidence him being here,' I said. 'Castellanos is in league with Thanos and this proves it as you can now see. I was right, but I'm also sorry. I've made a terrible mistake, poor judgement and worst of all...I've failed.'

'No, Mr. Fox,' said Christos. 'You tried. You tried for Mama and me and Philo. That is what is most important. Now we go back to the Aeres for free drinks on me. We should, how the English say, give three cheers for Jimmy Finn.'

'Three cheers for the free drinks,' Madge mumbled.

All the way back I worried, expecting Castellanos to be at the hotel waiting for me, despite Thanos' departing words. Thanos was gone and I didn't trust Castellanos to listen. Madge pestered me all the way, asking how I knew about Thanos' departure, where he was going and why the hell did I think it clever to get involved. Madge read me like a book. She knew I was leaving something out, that my 'hunch' explanation didn't make sense. I couldn't tell them about Balakros yet. Christos and I still had no plan for him. I'd counted on Thanos missing his passage and we could safely hand him over to some international agents...or something.

Back at the hotel I pulled Christos to one side. 'I'll try phoning Dreyfus again,' I said. 'God knows what he'll think of all this. I mean I'll have to confess everything from the start. But at least he should know what to do.'

'I would like to drop Balakros in the ocean,' said Christos. 'He cares nothing for us. He is a back-stabber, a double-crosser as Jimmy Finn would say.'

'I'd let you if I thought we could get away with it.'

So I rang Dreyfus. I rang and rang and rang again.

Evening came and I was getting edgy and tipsy after Christos' free drinks and running out of excuses for Madge and Mabel as to how we knew about Thanos departure. An hour, two drinks and four attempted phone calls later I noticed Christos had disappeared from the bar. I went outside looking for him.

At the end of the drive two dark figures were approaching.

29.

'I'm sorry, Mr. Fox,' said Christos. 'I saw the car and was curious. I went to see. He says he knows you.'

I knew him. I held out my hand. 'Adam Dreyfus? You came out. You ignored my calls, but came out here?'

Dreyfus loosened his tie and undid the top button of his smart blue shirt. The jacket was already thrown over the shoulder. 'Well, I didn't come for the heat.'

He held out his free hand. We shook and I invited him inside. Madge and Mabel stood up like he was an ambassador. Even with a jacket off, loose collar and wet armpits, Dreyfus always looked important. He had the square jaw of Dick Tracy, the inquiring gaze of James Stewart and the handshake of Popeye after a can of spinach. He was copper through and through, but not Castellanos copper. Dreyfus was copper-bottomed copper, solid and incorruptible and here in Gouvia. I could stop thinking about Castellanos.

We took a seat and Dreyfus explained. 'I acted once you told me about Castellanos. I didn't believe it at first, but there is another insider out here who sort of backed your story up. He knew about Castellanos' cheap bullying of hoteliers and bar owners and I thought...well, maybe this guy Castellanos has been bought and your instinct was right. And that photo. Once it came back as an identity I knew something was going on. I couldn't tell you any more at the time, but I passed your info on. The operation had already started.'

'Already started?' I said.

'I'm talking Interpol. We've been working with them and feeding information to police agencies of several interested countries. A helicopter was scrambled from the mainland, they acted quickly once we realised that information might be getting back to Thanos. Your instinct was right. He booked a flight he never intended taking. We believe Castellanos informed Thanos the net was closing and had the intention of pleading innocent later and pretending he knew nothing about his escape. But we have others, as I've said. We knew about the sea departure, but we couldn't tell you. That would have been disclosure of the operation which was closely guarded.'

'That must be why he took off so fast after seeing that helicopter,' said Madge. 'He didn't want to be seen there if he was going to deny knowing about the escape.'

'You got here pretty quick,' I said. 'It's not twenty-four hours since we last spoke on the phone.'

'I didn't have to come, but I really wanted to see and hear a bit more about how you figured out Castellanos was colluding with Thanos. I got lucky. There was a flight a few hours after your call so I jumped to it. I wasn't ignoring your calls, I just missed them.'

'What about the helicopter, was that you guys then?'

'You guys?' said Dreyfus. 'Those were agents from the Greek mainland acting on Interpol's information. I'm only involved in the intelligence side of the operation. I'm here mainly because I was worried about you.'

'Thanos thought the helicopter was one of his pickups,' I said. 'And what about Thanos himself? He said nobody would ever trace him. He had a gun on me at the time, by the way.'

'Relax. Thanos was intercepted. We have him in custody. Unfortunately Castellanos has disappeared and has a warrant out for his arrest. We've already arrested his junior officer, Eleftherios, I think it's pronounced.'

'Just say Deet, it's easier.'

'Pardon?'

'I'll explain later.'

'Anyway, he's helping us with enquiries,' said Dreyfus. 'Which now brings me to the question of why you thought it was okay to put other lives in danger? What you did was a waste of time and dangerously stupid. The chopper guys wondered what the hell that roadblock was all about. I heard they nearly aborted the mission when they saw what was happening on the ground. I'll thank you for the tip-off on Castellanos, it was one thing you did right. The rest was cavalier, reckless and stupid. You've got some serious explaining to do, Angelo. You can start by telling me how the hell you knew when and from where Thanos was leaving.'

'Yes, we'd like to know that too,' said Madge. 'He's been very stupid and acting totally out of character, he was, wasn't he, Mabel?'

'Out of character,' repeated Mabel. 'We tried to talk some sense into him, but sometimes the Jimmy Finn in him just doesn't listen to common sense.'

'I see,' said Dreyfus. 'Is that what you were doing, Angelo? Jimmy Finn could have cost lives and the world the apprehending of an international criminal.'

I explained it all. The whole story, nothing less and if Dreyfus laughed, cried, decided to arrest me or just punch me in the face, I didn't care anymore. I was simply that relieved he was here. I recapped on what I tried to tell him over the telephone, all the strange goings-on in Gouvia. Then, worried as I was about admitting it, I got to the break-in at Thanos' mansion, being arrested, jailed, and the story of the pants on fire. All the while, Dreyfus face never betrayed his thoughts. He was like that. As steely-faced as a poker player. It used to worry me back then when I was asking him what I thought might be stupid questions about police work for my writing research. Back then he would wait until I'd finished the question before reacting. In the meantime that deadpan face terrified me. I worked my way through the whole story, right the way through to Balakros.

Dreyfus was up into his car and on his CB handset in a flash. Agents were informed. We didn't wait; Christos had the

191

Rover out within two minutes with Dreyfus following close behind.

A few hours in the dark and in bonds hadn't softened Balakros' temper.

'You bastards, leaving me like this!' he yelled as soon as the gag was untied.

'I left you water and food,' said Christos.

'I need afodeyoun!'

'What does he mean?' I said.

'He needs to take a shite,' said Christos.

'Oh. We never thought of that.'

Christos cut his chair and foot bonds, leaving his hands still tied behind his back and led him upstairs.

Two mainland Greek agents arrived at the house soon after. Christos retrieved Balakros' blood money envelopes and the bag of plastic phials from its hiding place and handed them over. They cut Balakros' bonds, let him have a shite, cuffed him and disappeared into the night. I didn't mean to be poetic. That's just the order it happened.

'I'm following,' said Dreyfus. 'I want to hear what this one has to stool...pardon the pun. I'll be in touch. Someone will be with you in a day or two to finalise any explanations.'

Dreyfus left, Christos and I returned to the Aeres. Everyone had retired for the night. No guests, no Madge or Mabel. We had a peaceful nightcap with only a few whispered words. The most peaceful nightcap I'd had all holiday.

Holiday?

30.

Breakfast time. Croissants, omelette or Madeira cake? Any. Nothing tasted or smelled so good as the taste or smell of freedom. Especially when everything seems normal and peaceful. We were back at our usual table, Elena and the boys were busy serving and the new guests, although diminished in number, were chatty and happy, looking forward to a day on the beach, a day by the pool or a day searching the shops for identifiable food.

'I love the smell of Madeira cake in the morning,' I said.

'Are you quite alright?' said Madge. 'Where did that come from?'

'I'm sorry, it's a film misquote.'

'Understandable. You're just letting it all out from the relief. It's good to know the resort is safe at least.'

'So, it seems we were right all along?' said Mabel. 'About the shifty-looking little man, I mean.'

'Oh yes,' I said. 'Balakros was as bent as a three pound note. I apologise for not explaining it earlier. We needed time to figure out what to do with him. Anyway, I don't fancy his fate in the hands of those agents. Tough as nails they looked. I think they'll get their information I've no doubt.'

'And you have a story now', said Madge.

'I can't wait to read it,' said Mabel.

'You already know the story,' I said.

'Oh, how wonderful! Are we going to be in it?'

I didn't answer. Kevin appeared in the dining room for the keys to the Jeep. He sat down at our table and Christos brought him coffee and cake.

'I could have died,' said Kevin. 'I really thought I was going to.'

'Are the rest of the party alright?' I said.

'Terrified,' said Kevin. 'They daren't say or do anything. They don't even want to go out today. They're all laid out by the pool trying to unwind. That copper really put the shits up them. That's what really annoys me. You were breaking the law and risking our safety. And now we have this big ugly police chief who's gonna come and get us at anytime, if he thinks we've told anyone about yesterday. What the fuck were you playing at?'

'Relax,' I said. 'Castellanos is a wanted criminal now. There's a warrant out for him. He's the one that was breaking the law. I was only breaking Castellanos' law, which is corrupt law. You guys can say what you want. In fact there will be some agents here soon who no doubt will want to question you about the events. Tell them everything, don't worry about Castellanos, he'll be behind bars before you know it. I'm sorry, by the way. I honestly didn't expect things to pan out the way they did.'

'He held a gun at my head,' said Kevin. 'A fucking gun.'

'I had noticed.'

'Don't be so flippant about it.'

'Sorry again,' I said. 'If it's any consolation, what happened resulted in an internationally wanted criminal being apprehended. And you are all contributors. You're all heroes, in fact.'

'Really?'

'Really.'

'Well, I'm not sure about...' Mabel started, then squeaked like someone had kicked her under the table.

'Actually,' said Kevin, 'It was a bit different and if I'm honest, I quite enjoyed the rush...I mean once the danger was gone and that smelly copper had disappeared. It was a bit of fun. It kind of gave me an idea for a beach activity with the guys. I'm thinking of drafting a 'hostage' themed party sometime. You know, with pretend gangsters and coppers and plastic water pistols. One of the girls gets kidnapped, bundled in a Jeep and takes off to an unknown beach. The rest of the gang has to figure out where she is from some given clues and set off in pursuit after the kidnapper's head start. What do you think, Angelo?

'Oops, gun, at your head?'

Kevin didn't like that.

31.

Dreyfus called again two days later. I was out lounging by the pool at the time. Madge and Mabel had gone into Gouvia souvenir shopping for friends back home, having decided they were heading home in a day or two, not wanting to face any questioning about the Thanos affair. 'If they want me they can talk to me from the safety of my own sofa,' Madge had said. 'Sofa,' Mabel had repeated. He appeared through the fretwork arch of hibiscus, pulled up a deck chair and sat next to me. I sat up and was all ears.

'Here's the case with Thanos,' said Dreyfus 'The mansion Liontari Ilion had already been sold. All its valuables, including some extremely valuable and previously thought to have been lost or destroyed paintings had been either transferred to a South American country or sold off to criminal connections. And a lot of gold made that trip as well.'

'Makes sense now,' I said. 'The mansion was suspiciously bare inside when I saw it.'

'And that's where he made his fatal error. The captain of that yacht to collect Thanos from Heliakos was also involved in the transport of his cargo to South America. Some weeks ago a previously unseen vessel docked in a remote fishing village some miles from Buenos Aries. It seems the Port Master there was a fiddler, someone who took backhanders for waiving docking levies and turning a blind eye to minor smuggling. Seeing this out of the ordinary yacht in his little port, he must have realised the cargo was likely something bigger than booze or the usual local drug smuggling. He must have got a whiff of its value and wanted a cut. The crew were Thanos' contacts. They don't do deals with chancers. The Port Master got eliminated, but there was a witness who informed the local police. Now the local guys were equally as bent, routinely ignoring the port business. But one of them got scared and let out to Interpol. Interpol can't make arrests in a foreign country. They can, as in this case work with agents of the country where the criminal is wanted. We just had to know where he was located. Argentine Federal Intelligence Agents seized the cargo and its crew.

'And where was this cargo ultimately destined?'

'We're working on that,' said Dreyfus. 'Somewhere safe, somewhere it could be exchanged for hard currency, washed and banked in Thanos' new hideout. Thanos won't talk, but one of his crew might, if given an incentive.'

'Incentive?' I said.

'We'll cut a deal for amnesty with any that's willing to talk. That's what we did with the yacht's captain, who was previously a legitimate businessman facing a long prison sentence if he didn't help. He gave the info about the cargo's country of origin and he also agreed to cooperate when he was due to collect Thanos for his Argentina passage in exchange for an amnesty. His yacht left the Argentine port with a swapped crew of German Federal and Israel Foreign Intelligence agents. The only thing the agents didn't know was who Thanos really was, where exactly he lived and what he currently looked like...until your photo. The yacht's captain didn't even know that.'

'So the captain didn't even know who he was working for?'

'No he didn't,' said Dreyfus. 'The only instructions the criminals gave him were time, place and underworld names, fake names, of course. That's how they work, pay the runner that offer they can't refuse and keep them in the dark. The name Thanos was unknown to the captain.'

'How did you know about Thanos previously then?' I said. 'I mean before I contacted you.'

'Hector Thanos has been of interest to us for some time. We found that Thanos had wanted to develop a new tourist complex for the ultra-rich client. He'd bought up many properties in Corfu with the idea in mind. But some just stubbornly refused to sell and he never got the planning permission. His portfolio was too scattered for his plans. He'd wanted to buy up all the select areas and have them replaced with this ultra-tourist Mecca attracting only the cultured type of person, the best of society, he'd called it in his applications. Having failed, that's when he started selling off and transferring funds to several South American accounts. That's not illegal, but it is suspicious. That's when the banks passed on information, something they do if they think transactions may have criminal intent. Then we got the info about the murder and the yacht in the Argentine port. If Thanos hadn't tried to shift anything material he'd have stayed under radar and we probably would never have caught him. But something spooked him, forced him to make that move to a safe country. I think somehow he must have sensed that his actions were being monitored, and that his fake identity was in jeopardy. He was getting old and took one last chance to go somewhere he could simply disappear. He had other passports on him when we picked him up. A whole new identity and life, or so he thought.'

'But why would he want to run?' I said.

'Because his real name is Gerhard Katriuk,' said Dreyfus.

The name didn't strike any chords, other than it wasn't Greek. I was still puzzling over why Dreyfus had mentioned German and Israeli Federal agents? The gun Thanos had wasn't Greek either, if there was such a thing as a Greek made gun. He had a Luger. I could probably have figured the rest out by myself given time.

But I asked anyway. 'What are you trying to say?'

'Katriuk was a war criminal, a Nazi concentration camp officer once known as 'The Panther.' He wasn't nice either. He was known as a tormentor who had a penchant for petrol dousing and taunting with flaming rags until prisoners went out of their minds and threw themselves onto the wire perimeters. He got a kick out of it. Interesting the alias he picked for himself as well, the name Hector. Hector is classic Greek for 'one who holds fast' and Thanos means 'the immortal one.''

'I see it now,' I said. 'It all falls into place. The Panther? Appropriate, I suppose. I get the connection to Liontari Ilion and his obsession with owning a big cat. And the disruption in Gouvia. It was him. He was getting revenge for those that refused to sell up. He was still getting a kick out of human suffering. He must have really missed the old job. The immortal one, eh? Arrogant. He must have thought he was untouchable.'

'It certainly seems that way,' said Dreyfus. 'But he got too smart with his ambitions, this desire to re-profile the resort with a higher order of resident. That's typical Nazi ideology. He had enough wealth and should have kept his head down. But that's how they expose themselves, they can't help it.'

'How did he get here in the first place and not South America?' I said. 'That's where most of them absconded to, isn't it?'

'An interesting story. Our Israeli contacts have enlightened us on this one. After the war, Vatican officials tried to aid Catholic refugees fleeing the rise of communist regimes across Europe. In doing so they also unwittingly aided in the escape of Nazi war criminals, some of who had fled into Italy. Believing them to be Catholic refugees, the Vatican issued them false identity documents that were then used to obtain passports from the International Red Cross. Some clerics actually did so with full knowledge of their actions. They even collaborated in the shipment of their stolen goods. Thirty pieces of silver, as the saying goes. That's how Katriuk got out. Interestingly, that's how the infamous Adolf Eichmann got away as well. He had an Argentine visa and a signed application supplied by a Franciscan monk for his falsified Red Cross passport. It allowed him to board a steamship to Buenos Aires in 1950 under the assumed identity of Ricardo Klement. Most of the Nazis who entered the continent did so using forged Red Cross passports. They reckon hundreds of SS members fled that way to Argentina alone. Katriuk thought he was being smart by being in the woods you can't see for all the trees. It worked. Nobody knew him here, this quiet little island.'

'So some actual Vatican officials were bribed by the Nazis?' I said. 'It makes Castellanos' little free meals racket look almost innocent.'

'Castellanos?' said Dreyfus. 'He was more than just a paid stooge to cover Thanos. That's enough to haul him in, but he's also complicit in the escape of an international criminal.'

'Do you think he knew who Thanos really was?'

'No chance. Katriuk wouldn't risk that. To Castellanos he was just another rich guy offering him a meal ticket. We're looking at Castellanos' accounts as we speak. Some of that cash Balakros had stashed at his place was destined for Castellanos. Balakros confessed to it. They were payments for turning a blind eye to Katriuk's bullies trying to edge out the hoteliers here. We're close to proving it. He'll go down for a long stretch once he's captured.'

Another car pulled into the hotel drive and I momentarily panicked. It was a big car with a big guy stepping out. Another figure emerged from the car. They were heading for reception, but Dreyfus called them over. The big guy came through the arch first.

'Someone here I thought you might like to see,' he said.

I was on my feet before the other guy came through.

'Hello, Mr. Fox,' said Tobias.

I marched over with a smile bigger than a six-year old with a new bike and threw my arms around him.

Tobias was crying. I think I might have cried but never admitted it after. Big man hugs aren't my usual thing, but falsely accused and freed prisoners definitely are.

'You did this, Mr. Fox,' said Tobias. 'You got me out. I will never be able to repay you.'

Dreyfus briefly introduced the big guy, whose name I forget but didn't matter much. Apparently he was a big guy in size and a big guy in police internal affairs on the island investigating the shabby affairs of Castellanos. The other insider Dreyfus had mentioned. I couldn't have cared less at that given moment.

'Enjoy the rest of your holiday and keep in touch when you get home,' said Dreyfus. And then they were off. I hardly heard them leave.

'Do Elena and the boys know you're here?' I said.

'Not yet,' said Tobias. 'I'm going to surprise them soon.'

'So what happened?'

'The man who has just left, he came for me with a 'warrant' is it? He said Castellanos' evidence is flawed. Balakros has confessed and they let me go.'

'He's confessed?' I said. 'I knew it wouldn't take long. The little shit was a coward and sucker for Castellanos. So what has he said exactly?'

'He said he was wiping plates with the poison. He also spread some sickness to other hotels, he said this. They told him they would go easy on him if he told everything. Castellanos said this to me, to make me confess to poisoning Mr. Barton, but he was lying. Balakros told the warrant man

201

he had to do these things because he was afraid of some mafiosos in Corfu.'

'And for the money, of course,' I said. 'That's the real reason, I think.'

'Castellanos, he hid the poison in my room after Balakros spread it on one of the soup dishes in the morning. It was unfortunate for me because the dish went to Mr. Barton's table. Because Mr. Barton was bullying me, Castellanos used this to frame me for murder and make it look like he was doing good police work. The warrant man, he also said Balakros put something in a boat and made it blow up. I didn't understand what this thing was. He said it was 'sodium,' but I thought sodium was what we have in the hotel, you know...salt. He tried to explain.'

'I'll tell you about it later, Tobias. I'll explain it all and how it made my pants explode.'

'Pardon, Mr. Fox?'

'Let's just go surprise Elena, Christos and Philo for now, shall we? Philo might explain it better than me anyway.'

It was a surprise alright, one that turned into a big party and everyone was invited. Elena could hardly stop crying for an hour. Well she did actually, for a few minutes at a time in between preparing for the evening meal and then started again hardly believing that her favourite other son had come back to the nest. Life always goes on in the Samaras household.

Madge and Mabel couldn't understand what was going on when they entered the dining room, then screamed with delight at the sight of Tobias. Evening meal was served, helped by a delighted Tobias who kept introducing himself to each of the new guests who still didn't understand the celebrations. Explaining would be complicated, especially about being an ex-prisoner, so Tobias just said he was the new guy, just hired and delighted he'd found his dream job at last. In the evening

Christos did a runner over to the 18-30 Club to spread the good news and invite Kevin and gang over for free drinks on the Aeres. A day on the beach chasing beer into the sea didn't deter them. I mean, free drinks? They were just getting started. And they behaved themselves. Maybe Castellanos' words were still having an effect.

And all too soon, it was over.

Home time was looming.

32.

In a couple of days Madge and Mabel packed up, having booked a flight home the day after Dreyfus' visit and Tobias' happy return. I could have done the same, but decided I needed another day or two of utter peace doing nothing but finalising the rough manuscript of my novel. So far ninety percent of it was still in my head. Scribbling it out for the agent waiting back home wouldn't take long if I was left alone.

I did, however, accompany Madge and Mabel to the airport. I hired a decent car for the occasion, this time a four-door. A nice clean Seat with nice clean seats.

We had final hugs at the Border Control with exchanged addresses and phone numbers and promises to meet up again in the near future. I handed Madge a personal cheque for one-thousand pounds.

'That's considerably more than I bribed Castellanos with,' said Madge.

'Late interest payment,' I said. 'I'd almost forgotten in all the confusion.'

'I would have reminded you in due course. And we'll be looking out for that novel, Angelo, won't we, Mabel?'

'Looking out for it alright,' said Mabel. 'We can't wait. I don't suppose we could be in it, could we?'

'I'll have to change a few things around to make it plausible,' I said. 'But I think there will be a 'based on a true story' note on the back cover. May I use your real names?'

'Silly,' said Madge. 'We fully expect you to do so.'

'You could probably make more than one story out of our adventures, couldn't you?' said Mabel.

'Actually,' I said. 'I've been thinking about that. My agent sounded disapproving of me making something Corfu based. He doesn't like it. He wants me to stick to the safe option of mysteries located in the wealthy English suburbs. But, I will write our story first. Then just to keep him sweet I've been thinking about another project after and our adventures have given me some inspiration. I've been considering a series of crime stories based on you two.'

'Oh, how wonderful,' said Mabel. 'What's it about?'

'Here's the idea: I've thought of creating two lady gardeners that work around the estates of the rich and famous that, for example, overhear more than they should in their daily duties, or stumble across the odd murder or extortion racket or drug manufacturing plant. Or perhaps a rich baron who is not what he seems and is actually a bigwig in the underworld. And these two unassuming ladies in their gardening dungarees with their spades and trowels manage to crack the case each time. What do you think?'

'And here's me thinking you were just talking about making it plausible,' said Madge. 'I mean, two elderly lady gardener crime fighters? What would you even call them?'

'I was thinking of something gardening related. Something like, Parsley and Sage.'

Mabel frowned at me like I'd spoken Latin. Madge leaned on her shoulder and sighed. I shrugged my shoulders. They burst out laughing.

'Parsley and Sage!' Madge squealed.

'Two elderly gardeners called Parsley and Sage!' said Mabel.

'Well, maybe not those particular names,' I said. 'Perhaps Rosemary and some other herb related name might work together better. It's just an idea.'

'Two elderly lady gardeners named after herbs that go around gardening and solving crimes.' said Madge. 'Have you heard yourself, Angelo? Oh dear, I really think you've had too long in the sun. Go back to the hotel, have a stiff drink and a lie down. We'll see you back in the UK soon.'

'Have a lie down,' repeated Mabel.

They both waved me at Passport Control.

And then they were gone.

I drove back to the Aeres, had a stiff drink and didn't lie down. I did some work on the manuscript, didn't go anywhere and suddenly felt like the archetypal reclusive writer. I went to bed early.

The next morning after breakfast I took my notes out to the pool, now quiet. The pool was empty for cleaning. Christos was cheerful having pole-netted no picnic bars. He and Philo scrubbed it and hosed it ready for refilling from the sea. It was as empty as my heart. I had two days left. There was maybe one thing that might help. I still had the hire car for another day.

I took a drive out to Liontari Ilion. To this day I'm not sure why. I told myself it was to get a better picture of the place for my book. Maybe it was really to try and make sense of the past days.

I pulled up and parked outside the steel gate. It was no longer locked and left ajar an inch. It squeaked a little as I pushed it open just enough to squeeze through. The place looked a little different, mainly the flower beds that drooped from lack of watering. A melancholy breeze from the ocean hissed along the grass, rustling the leaves in the trees and foliage. I hadn't noticed it on my first visit. I wasn't fretting about meeting a millionaire property developer this time. I had a good mosey around, wondering what would eventually happen to the place. That writer's retreat idea I'd lied about seemed plausible, but someone like a writer would have to buy it. It wasn't on and I was kidding myself.

I wandered around the back of the mansion among the citrus trees and ornamental shrubs. Near the bottom wall there was a vineyard I hadn't noticed from inside the house before. I turned and looked at the rear of the building. It was a lonely place when Thanos occupied it, even lonelier now. I still thought of him as that name – Thanos. Gerhard Katriuk was a stranger from the distant past I felt like I'd never met. Thanos was the name I knew, the man I knew, or thought I knew.

This was the side of the property that hadn't been renovated, not brought up to date with contemporary architectural design. I imagined the patients of the former war hospital, arising from bed for the first time and seeing the blue sky of Corfu and what a delight it must have been after the horrors of war.

I could daydream all day, but I had work to do before leaving the island. I started heading back round to the front. Half way round the side of the building I was hit from behind, suddenly and hard in the leg. My knee buckled, sending me to the lawn face first. I rolled over quickly to see a familiar face.

'Hello Charlie.'

Charlie was purring. He rubbed his beautiful muzzle against my leg like he was apologising for the unannounced greeting. The last time he'd rubbed against me like that was two minutes before he slaughtered a piglet in spectacular fashion. I was nervous, but not like before. I realised Charlie could have struck me down as a primordial killer as easily as he had the piglet. He could have done it again, the night I sneaked into these same grounds. But he didn't. Charlie had remembered me. I reached out my hand, a little more confidently than last time we met. He head-bumped my fist and flopped down on his side, stretching out that deadly paw that could slash me to ribbons and pushed it into my belly gently. His claws dug a little, but didn't break skin and didn't hurt too much. I figured he was hungry. He was affectionate like this just before the pig hunt. I reckoned he was telling me something.

Charlie had something new about him. He had a collar that wasn't there last time. On the neck of it was a clasp, a locket with a catch. I felt it as Charlie purred, rolled and pawed me like I was his mother. Carefully I snapped the catch and fingered out the note inside. It was written in both Greek and English.

"My name is Charlie," it read. "If found..." Then there was some crossing out in the English version. "When you find me, please deliver me to the wildlife sanctuary at Paleos. I was born there. My brothers are there. I came from there. Angelo, I know you will return. That is in your nature, the curiosity of the writer, the true adventurer. If you return to Liontari Ilion, I know Charlie will find you. I am sorry I had to leave Charlie. I hope you are the first to find him. Deliver him for me please.'

Now I realised why Thanos wanted Castellanos to leave me alone. I doubted he'd trust Castellanos to deliver Charlie to the Sanctuary. I wasn't sure if Castellanos even knew about Charlie. He would have noticed Charlie on the photos he confiscated, but never mentioned it at the time. I guessed he had other things on his mind. Like getting hold of that one snap of Thanos.

I thought about leaving Charlie, finding a phone and getting the police. They would arrive armed and most likely shoot Charlie. I'm sure they would. Charlie didn't deserve that. Thanos did. I'd shoot Thanos myself. I didn't owe Thanos anything. I respected him in a warped sort of way and hated him at the same time. I hated him even more for leaving Charlie. I didn't owe him or Charlie any favours. Maybe Charlie. At least he liked me. At least he hadn't eaten me. I owed Charlie for that and for trying to drug him.

I got up and Charlie followed me. 'Come on, Charlie. Let's see if we can find you something to eat.'

Charlie followed me around to the front of the mansion and up the left stairway. The door was shut but not locked. I pushed it open and walked in to an eerily silent hallway that echoed the creaking door. It wasn't much different. The piano was gone, but the giant pots remained with withered plants.

Thanos had moved mostly everything he wanted before we'd first met. I led Charlie through the hallway, the reception room and downstairs to the kitchen. We were in luck. One of the fridges had a joint in it. I think it was beef. I took it out and offered it Charlie. He sniffed and licked it, but didn't grab.

'I get it, Charlie. Come on then.'

Charlie followed me back upstairs, sniffing the joint all the way. He trotted at my side back through the hall and out onto the front drive, his tail stuck straight up like any other house cat about to get a meal. He purred loudly, knowing what was coming. I held the joint two-handed, swung it back and forth and launched it as far as I could down the mosaic drive, the blood splattering the colourful pattern into red patches, defiling it. It was pleasing to do that. Not pleasing to defile any artwork, but defiling what Thanos had built. Charlie took the cue and launched himself into full pelt. It all took about two seconds and he spilled across it just like it was a piece of live game. He laid his paws across it a few seconds, picked it up and disappeared just like he had with the piglet around the side of the mansion.

I sat and waited on a remaining wicker chair in the shade of the veranda, daydreaming and dozing about an hour, maybe, not thinking about the past or writing, just waiting and trying to figure out what to do about Charlie.

I don't know quite what it was, but Charlie had taught me something in our short friendship, something ethereal, being around him. Maybe some of that primordial awareness or perception transcends the species between man and beast, that instinct when things are not right. For me it was something simpler. The stink of cigar. Whether lit or not, I knew its scent and its owner. Cigar and sweat smell like corruption. Corruption in Corfu had that same smell. Sweat and cigar.

'Well, well, well...Mr. Derek Plumpton.' The voice from behind was gentle and mocking. He must have already been in the building or the garden, hiding out and come either from the entrance or the right-hand stairs. Either way, it didn't matter. Castellanos was there behind me. Not close, but close enough for the back breeze to drift his stink by.

I was tempted to spin around in the chair, but I didn't. I knew he was there and played it cool, pretending I didn't. I got up slowly, listening for movement. I walked a couple of steps to the edge of the veranda, stretching, yawning and pretending to admire the view.

Castellanos raised his voice: 'You seem to be a little deaf, Plumpton.'

I turned slowly. Castellanos had a gun holstered at his hip. I guessed it was legit. Even Greek cops had access to guns in certain situations. Being a desperately wanted criminal on the run was one.

'Rather naive, isn't it?' I said. 'Coming back here of all places?'

'I think I'm in exactly the right place,' said Castellanos. 'These so-called agents are the naive ones to think they can track me. They already have been here looking for me, I can tell this because I am a wise detective who knows these things by instinct. So I am now quite safe here until things settle down. Then I will quietly leave this island. Hector Thanos has promised me a passage soon from a secret place and a place somewhere safe in another country and a new identity. And now luck has it that I am here with the one who crossed me. No one crosses Elias Castellanos, especially a mere nobody like you, Mr. Derek Plumpton.'

'You realise that promise came from a man now in the hands of European and Israeli agents? And as for crossing you, I don't think so. Interpol already had their suspicions. I just helped them confirm it. Give yourself up man, it's over.'

'Goodbye Mr. Derek Plumpton.' He drew the gun.

Charlie appeared up the stairs behind. He trotted towards

me, his tail up like he was coming for a roll and a cuddle. But he didn't. He head nudged Castellanos along his right thigh. Castellanos spun round with a gasp of astonishment and stepped back. His heel overreached the top step. He hovered there a second, waving his arms desperately trying to regain his balance and went over backwards. He bounced first and twice cracked his head hard, before sliding down to the bottom like a walrus sliding off an ice floe, leaving blood splatters on the way.

I ran down to his side. He lay there face up, his legs still on the bottom few steps. A ring of blood slowly formed under his head and ran out onto the drive. I should have run for help. I could have run to the car and drove to the nearest village for help. But I didn't. It wouldn't have made any difference. Castellanos was still breathing, but losing blood too rapidly. Nothing I could do would save him. And he was going to shoot me.

Charlie padded his way down the stairs and sniffed at him. He didn't lick. Charlie didn't eat carrion, or any beast he hadn't killed or believed he'd killed. It's like he knew what had happened. He brushed his head against my shoulder as I sat watching Castellanos bleed. I think it was Charlie's way of apologising.

'For heaven's sake man, he only wanted to say hello,' I mumbled.

I let him bleed. He was out of it anyway, unconscious, without pain. I didn't touch him. It was callous, I know, as I waited and watched Castellanos' life slip away from him, like he'd watched Tobias sentenced to the Big House to rot his life away. Like he'd got his stooge Balakros to do Thanos' work to poison Barton. Like he'd covered for Thanos as he brought death and mayhem to a beautiful island resort.

I sat and waited until the last gargled breath stopped. I was going to leave him there, pretend I didn't know he was there. I hadn't seen anything. I couldn't pretend I hadn't been at the mansion, but I would deny having seen Castellanos. I checked my watch. I'd say I'd been there earlier. I didn't know anything about any dead body. Reporting it was too complicated. I was going to just walk away. I'd likely be home in the UK before Castellanos' body was discovered. I knew nothing.

And I had other business.

Charlie was grooming himself. He lay down at my side on the bottom step, licking a paw, wiping the beef blood from his face and purring even louder than before. I stroked him while I thought about things, resolved things in my mind. I thought about the Sanctuary, which I figured was about an hour's drive. Everywhere on Corfu was about an hour's drive. I could go there and tell them about Charlie, get them to come out and pick him up.

But I couldn't explain Castellanos.

I got up and Charlie followed. I went out to the car. I didn't know if Charlie liked cars. I hoped so. He must have come to Liontari Ilion in some vehicle at some time. Sometime when he was a cub.

'Come on Charlie, hop in. I'm taking you home.'

Also by Andy Jarvis:

Isabel's Light:

What do a vicar, an archaeologist, a gardener, two workmen and a dark, skulking figure that hides behind walls and under hedges have in common? Not a lot, unless you include murder, witchcraft, mystery and the supernatural. Ed and Baz are contract workers unwittingly digging up something they just weren't meant to find. Ever curious, adventurous and sometimes downright reckless, the two best friends apply their unique brand of street wisdom to solve a ghostly crime mystery from the distant past. Haunting, darkly humorous and original.

Solway Tide:

DC Roberta Sharp is more than just your average police detective. Outspoken, sassy and determined to make it up through the ranks, she's assigned to follow the case of a body found in the sea only to find herself the one being pursued. Far from being a run-of-the-mill murder tale this gripping page turner takes the genre by the horns throwing it in a totally new direction. A nightmare of a tale that challenges the very philosophy and motivation behind genetic experimentation and what possibly could be the 'hidden agenda' behind modern medical research. A setting on the remote west coast of Cumbria provides an eerie, atmospheric, heath land backdrop to this imaginative, twisting story of murder, corruption and the darker side of human nature

The Ray Hunters:

Mila is a young African boy who finds his idyllic life shattered when his tribe cast him out for betraying a visiting merchant. Knowing nothing about the outside world of 1830, Mila naively sets off to find 'civilization' and the trader to atone for his crime. African corsairs, slave traders, a Spanish pirate girl, an evil travelling show owner and an English railway engineer are among the characters that mould Mila's perception of humanity on an incredible journey that will sweep the reader away to another time and place. An extraordinarily captivating story.

The Ray Pool: Mila and Julieta's Story

Part two of 'The Ray Hunters.' The continuing story of Mila and Julieta. Three years have passed since Mila and Julieta were reunited and travelled to their new life on the island of Kerkyra Having survived the horrors of the past, their simple lives with Trader and his new wife seem idyllic on their peaceful, secluded homestead away from the troubles of the outside world. But soon that idyll is under threat. Others from the past have learned of their whereabouts.

And one person in particular has not forgotten.

Murder by Precision

"I'd seen a gun like it. In the film Get Carter. A bad guy's gun. Two wide barrels hack-sawn to size along with the stock. A neat little homemade assassin's device you could slip down your pants and still walk down the street without limping. Both barrels looked me square in the eyes. I put my hands up. There was nothing in here I could grab and Drago could see it."

Engineers Jake and Charlie believe the death of a colleague crushed in an industrial machine was no accident and talk each other into doing their own investigation. Involving maverick private detective Ron Selby seems a good idea until they stumble on a drug distribution plant run by the director of a rival company. In too deep to back out of a bad situation, they use a combination of street-wisdom, Selby's expertise at digging out the truth and good luck to get to the bottom of a tense, darkly humorous and violent murder mystery.

FOOTNOTES:

The character Gerhard Katriuk is fictional. However, many of the Nazis who escaped to South America were never brought to justice. SS colonel Walter Rauff, who created mobile gas chambers that killed at least 100,000 people, died in Chile in 1984. Eduard Roschmann, the "Butcher of Riga," died in Paraguay in 1977. Gustav Wagner, an SS officer known as the "Beast," died in Brazil in 1980 after the country's supreme federal court refused to extradite him to Germany because of inaccuracies in the paperwork. Perhaps the most notorious of the fugitives was Dr. Josef Mengele, the "Angel of Death" who conducted macabre experiments at the Auschwitz concentration camp was in various European locations before he fled to Argentina in 1949. He moved to Paraguay in 1959 and Brazil a year later. On 7 February 1979, while visiting his friends Wolfram and Liselotte Bossert in the coastal resort of Bertioga, Mengele suffered a stroke while swimming and drowned. His body was buried in Embu das Artes under the name "Wolfgang Gerhard," whose identification Mengele had been using since 1971.

The International Criminal Police Organization, commonly known as INTERPOL, is an international organization that facilitates worldwide police cooperation and crime control. It is the world's largest international police organization, headquartered in Lyon, France, with seven regional bureaus worldwide, and a National Central Bureau in all 195 member states.

Contrary to popular belief, INTERPOL can't make arrests in a foreign country. They can, as in this fictional case, send agents working from the country where they are wanted and trap them once they're in that area. A Red Notice is a request to law enforcement worldwide to locate and provisionally arrest a person pending extradition, surrender, or similar legal action. It is based on an arrest warrant or court order issued by the judicial authorities in the requesting country. Member countries apply their own laws in deciding whether to arrest a person.

A Red Notice contains two main types of information:

Information to identify the wanted person, such as their name, date of birth, nationality, hair and eye colour, photographs and fingerprints if available.

Information related to the crime they are wanted for, which can typically be murder, rape, child abuse, armed robbery, drug smuggling and war crimes.

Red Notices are published by INTERPOL at the request of a member country, and must comply with INTERPOL's Constitution and Rules.